THE CONSORTIUM

Crime fiction from the heart of Wales

NICOLA CLIFFORD

THE BOOK FOLKS

Published by The Book Folks

London, 2021

This book is a work of fiction. Names, characters, businesses, organizations, places and events are either the product of the author's imagination or are used fictitiously. Any resemblance to actual persons, living or dead, events or locales is entirely coincidental. The spelling is British English.

ISBN 978-1-913516-40-6

www.thebookfolks.com

Dedicated to Barrow Poets, Susan and William Bealby-Wright 1930-2020

Chapter one

Strange lights were often seen above the Epynt Mountain in Mid Wales. Most residents put them down to the Army practicing on the firing ranges; a few conspiracy theorists said aliens were responsible. This night, though, was different and locals knew they were in for a disturbed night's sleep.

Deep into the open countryside, a depression was filled with people – dancing, happy people. Coloured lights reflected on thin mist and cast bizarre shadows on gorse bushes and the odd section of drystone walling, the entire landscape bouncing in time with thumpingly loud, fast-tempo dance music. A sea of heads undulated beneath a dark, star-sprinkled sky; thousands of feet pounded the already flat grass and created a deep drumming sound. Some partygoers danced with their eyes shut, limbs flailing wildly, falling on others in the crowd who held them upright. Others merely swayed to the music, eyes glazed, watching the lights, the crowd and things only they could see. Many were holding cans of alcohol, some smoking spliffs, others out of their minds on magic mushrooms, ecstasy and worse.

The party had begun around eleven o'clock the previous evening. It was now a little after four on the morning of the 21st June, midsummer's day, longest of the year and the reason for the gathering. Attendees had travelled from miles around and were making the most of it. Penalties for arranging an event like this were now so harsh that there were fewer parties – fewer organisers were willing to put their necks on the line. The ones that did happen attracted hundreds, sometimes thousands. The majority of the crowd had been dancing since the start and didn't seem to have lost any of their enthusiasm, although the groups of sitting partygoers were growing larger. Some couples crept away in search of privacy, other lone souls collapsed where they had danced and lay on dewy grass, coated in sweat, breathless, waiting for the sun to crest above the mountains. Sunrise on the longest day.

Stacey Logan, reporter for *The Mid Wales Times*, had arrived a couple of hours ago and although she hadn't come to dance, she found herself entangled by the happy horde, their smiles infectious, the friendly atmosphere addictive. But Stacey didn't have enough stamina to dance longer than an hour. Discovering a large boulder on a rise overlooking the site, she leant against the rough surface and took the occasional photo. This story would certainly make the paper.

The sky gradually lightened, music slowed and an excited anticipation fizzled on the breeze. More tribe members ceased their dancing and gazed at the ridge, watched for the pinking of the sky heralding the approach of the sun. At the exact moment the paper-thin crescent first topped the mountains, every fist in the field pumped the air to greet the new day. Dancers cheered and whooped, hugging each other, kissing strangers and the music returned to its previous volume. Stacey clicked away with her camera, a large smile curling her lips.

A young couple ran past laughing, hand in hand. They were wobbly on their feet, but whether that was due to a night of dancing, drugs or beer, Stacey couldn't tell and she sidestepped as they lurched towards her. The lad mumbled his apologies as he bumped her with his shoulder, before they were lost in the early morning mist and the last night shadows.

Stacey hauled herself up to the top of the rock and gazed around. The nearest metalled road – a narrow lane – was about half a mile away and she spotted an assortment of vehicles parked above the shallow valley. Something was moving slowly behind the row of stationary cars and vans. Using binoculars, she made out a second line of traffic, the local constabulary on its way to party-poop, and although the dancers didn't know it yet, some of them were about to lose their smiles, and possibly their liberty.

* * *

DI Ben James and DS Jack Trent climbed out of the first car and waited for the convoy of vans to park and disgorge their contents, a large contingent of uniformed officers with a fair smattering of PCSOs.

Ben stood on top of a high verge and addressed the group.

'Good morning, hope you're all awake. We've handled this sort of thing before – some of you will remember the event a couple of years ago. As always, we will go in gently and suggest the ravers leave. Don't go marching over there with batons drawn, shouldn't be necessary, but if asking nicely fails, we will have to encourage a little harder.'

Officers in the squad muttered, a few chuckled, nervous with anticipation.

Ben continued. 'Keep your eyes open for any drug dealing and don't hesitate to nick the perpetrators, but don't nick anyone for swearing at you or calling you names.' Ben paused for effect. 'Think of the paperwork!'

A few of his audience laughed and nodded sagely.

'OK then, boys and girls, form two groups. I'll head one, DS Trent the other, and remember, as little fuss as possible.'

The hundred strong force strode across open grassland and headed for the natural depression. Stacey spotted them and remained on her rock to record proceedings. Early morning light shone on dark ranks of police and she thought they resembled a tribe. She imagined the officers carrying spears and wearing feathered headdresses, and giggled to herself. Outlying dancers soon spotted the approaching horde. News rippled through the crowd which split into several small groups as people tried to move out of the way of any potential trouble. The drug dealers vanished first, as though they had melted into the grass and bracken. Some of the younger partygoers stood their ground, convinced they weren't committing any crime, but the more seasoned amongst them scattered, anxious not to spend the remainder of the night in a police cell. A group of about thirty heckled the cops from the sidelines, shouting insults, and a few lobbed empty cans and bottles.

The teams were ready for them. DS Trent ordered his group to head for the troublemakers, batons drawn. A rowdy group of dancers congregated around a particularly vocal lad, joined in his taunting chant and wound up the officers. In seconds the two groups clashed and scuffles broke out. A constable was knocked off his feet and quickly vanished in a forest of legs. Jack Trent was close by, grabbed hold of the man's collar, dragged him upright, and then pushed on through the rabble rousers to snatch the ringleader. Jack ducked as the lad took a swing at him and countered with a hefty punch into a flabby belly. The youth's knees folded as the wind went out of him and he hit the grass.

'You're nicked, sunshine,' Jack growled, snapping handcuffs on the wriggling man and shoving him in the direction of waiting uniforms, who bundled him up the slope and into the back of a waiting van. Jack scanned the area and saw Ben wrestle another teenager to the ground, a uniformed officer wading in to assist. Jack took a deep breath, turned back to the main crowd and ploughed ahead, snagging a youth openly smoking cannabis and added another arrest to his record.

The rising sun had chased away the last of the night, the impromptu party and the music were over. A group of constables dismantled the sound system while being verbally harassed by the DJ and his crew, all of whom were standing in handcuffs looking miserable.

After a few hectic hours, the job was done, vans shuffled about in the lane and then set off towards the main police station in Builth Wells. DI James and DS Trent stood side by side on the verge and shared coffee from a flask. Stacey spotted them and hurried across the open ground to the lane.

'Morning, boys,' she called. 'Having fun?'

'Stacey!' Ben spun round. 'I don't need to ask why you're here, but how on earth did you manage to get here so fast?'

'By keeping my ears to the ground – and there's only one of me,' she said. 'Didn't have to whistle up a task force before I left home.' She perched on the bonnet of the nearest patrol car. 'Any comments to make for the press?' she asked cheekily and mimed licking a pencil she poised above an imaginary notebook.

Ben huffed. 'Not really, no, but I'm guessing you don't need me to say much. How long have you been here?'

'A few hours, got wind of the rave on the net and – as I wasn't far away – managed to get in before your boys in blue set up the road blocks. Don't think they made much difference though, do you? How many kids do you reckon were here?'

'Eight hundred or so,' Jack grumbled, 'don't know where they all came from. Why aren't they at home going slowly blind watching porn on their computers or sharing their shallow, insignificant lives on Facebook? That's what I'd like to know.'

'God, Jack, don't be such a grouch.' Stacey thumped him gently on the arm. 'You were young once and let's be honest, they were only dancing. Where's the harm in that?'

'We don't make the law, Stace, we merely uphold it and "raving" is illegal, has been since the passing of the Criminal Justice and Public Order Act 1994. "No more than twenty people can listen to music in the open air – unlicensed". Used to be a hundred.'

'You're like a walking law dictionary,' Stacey said with a laugh. 'Great event though, lovely atmosphere and there didn't appear to be any trouble – well, until you lot showed up, that is. Any coffee left?'

'A little, here.' Ben held out a plastic cup.

Stacey mumbled her thanks. 'Are you coming over this evening?'

'Should be,' Ben said. 'We've got all day to process the kids we've nicked, so I should be able to get away early evening.'

'Good.' Stacey drained the dregs of the lukewarm liquid and handed back the cup. 'Gotta go, Sherlock, front page to write and if it's not with Sam by lunch, he'll be after my hide.' She pecked him quickly on the cheek, patted Jack on his shoulder and set off across country, heading for her cottage in the nearby village of Llanagethin.

Chapter two

Ben and Stacey sat together at the kitchen table and shared a supper of lasagne and fresh green salad.

'You look tired, love,' Stacey said.

'Early starts always do me in,' he muttered. 'This is gorgeous, Pumpkin, I've been looking forward to this all day.' He shovelled a large forkful of food into his mouth and chewed.

'Glad you like it. How many arrests then?' she asked.

'Twenty-one in all, four for drugs, four for making a racket, two resisting arrest, eleven cautioned. Most scarpered as soon as they saw us coming. Good job really, the cells are bursting. Felt sorry for poor old Geraint, the custody sergeant, he had his hands full, but all seemed to go well. We'll keep the magistrates busy tomorrow with ten in court. Would you like some more wine?'

Stacey nodded, Ben topped up her glass and refilled his own.

'Better make this the last for me,' he said, 'another early start in the morning. How about you?'

'Day off. I want to take a look at the rave site in proper daylight, now everyone's gone home.'

'Not going to court? You do surprise me.'

'No, new lad started, Andrew Carr, just out of uni, so Sam's sending him to dip his toes in.' She sipped from her glass. 'You know, Ben, I enjoyed myself out there this morning, lovely when the sun rose and everyone cheered, primeval somehow. What a shame events like that were banned.'

'Hardly surprising though, isn't it?' he asked. 'Not so great if it's your land these people are trashing; rubbish and human waste everywhere after a thing like that, and of course the drugs which always seem to be involved. Still, we managed to collar a couple of dealers, things may be quieter on the streets for a while.'

'Catching a few makes a difference to the supply, does it?'

'Depressingly, not really and not for long. There are always more to take their place, a new generation of kids who think dealing drugs is an easy way to get rich, when we all know it isn't.' Ben pushed his plate away, groaning. 'I'm stuffed! Nothing for it but a DVD until bedtime. You go and choose one, I'll see to the dishes and we can relax. I'm bushed and supper finished me off.'

* * *

The next morning the couple shared a pot of coffee before Ben headed off to Llandrindod Wells for the session at court, having arranged to meet his sergeant there. After his car pulled away, Stacey collected the paper from the front doormat and sat at the kitchen table to read, sipping another strong coffee. The long day yesterday was still having repercussions and she yawned.

The Mid Wales Times – 22nd June
ILLEGAL RAVE ON MOD LAND by Stacey Logan

Twenty-one people were arrested in the early hours of the 21st June, on MoD land close to the village of Garth, just off the A483, Llandovery road.
In a large operation, more than 100 officers worked with the military and local authorities to minimise disruption to the local community. Roads leading to the site were blocked by police in an effort to stop people gaining access to the area, but over 800 partygoers managed to attend. The rave was stopped soon after sunrise with only a few minor scuffles and no injuries. Eleven individuals were released with a police caution, four charged with drugs related offences, the remainder – due to appear at the magistrates' court – were charged with offences under the Criminal Justice and Public Order Act 1994.

A good-sized picture accompanied the article, clearly showing the site and ranks of police officers marching purposefully towards the dancers. The photo had printed well and Stacey was satisfied. Folding the paper she trotted upstairs, showered and dressed. Walking out to the car, she dumped her daysack on the back seat and drove through the winding lanes towards the Garth site.

* * *

The magistrates' court began on time and one by one the accused were dealt with. Two accused of drug offences were referred to Crown Court, one was remanded. Two others were handed community service orders, the organisers had their sound system confiscated and the rest were fined. The magistrate was efficient, and by half past one, all cases had been processed. Ben and Jack walked into hot, afternoon sunshine, pleased with their efforts.

'Fancy a bite of lunch before we head back to Llandovery?' Ben asked. 'Thought we could call in at The Lakeside restaurant on the edge of town. Nothing fancy, but they serve a decent steak and ale pie.'

'Good idea, boss,' Jack said. 'Watching all that justice meted out has certainly sharpened my appetite. I haven't been to The Lakeside before, thought about it, but never had the time.'

'We should treat ourselves, you did well yesterday. Remarkably trouble free, there have been some right old punch-ups in the past.' Ben unlocked the car.

Jack laughed. 'You should have seen some of the raves we had to contend with in London, all a bit of a game really. Gangs of kids hanging around service stations on the motorways, waiting for a tip-off, location of the next bash. They weren't subtle either, and as soon as one of them received a call, the place emptied as they all shot off to find the party. The ones we attended were usually held in empty warehouses and lots more people… lots of blood too when one of them really kicked off.'

Ben pulled into a parking space on the banks of the Victorian pleasure lake. 'Let's sit out by the water, we can feed the ducks. You find a table and I'll find a menu.'

They were finishing their second coffee when Ben's mobile chirped.

'DI James.' Ben listened intently, while Jack threw some bread crusts to a group of coots and swans which paddled past a large, metal dragon sculpture, half submerged beneath the water.

'What?' Ben asked. 'Say that again will you, sir?' He furrowed his brows. Jack watched him, interest pricked.

'Yes, I've got that. Where are you?' Ben listened again. 'I know. Wait on the lane, sir, we'll be there shortly.' Switching off the phone he turned to Jack. 'No rest for the wicked.'

'What's up, boss?'

'That was Gareth Hughes, hill farmer near Garth, the desk sergeant gave him my number. He's been out checking his land after the rave and has discovered a body.'

'A body?'

Ben nodded. 'Let's get over there. Gareth's called it in and an ambulance is on its way, but he's certain it's too late for that.'

'Where did he find the body?' Jack asked. 'We checked the area yesterday.'

Ben strode towards the car. 'Not well enough, it would seem; says he's discovered a young girl lying in a drainage ditch. You drive, we're in a hurry.'

DS Trent made good time and fifteen minutes later slid to a stop on loose gravel in the narrow lane overlooking the dance site. Gareth Hughes was sitting on his quad bike waiting for them and raised a hand as the car approached.

'You were fast, boys,' he said. 'Ambulance hasn't arrived yet. Follow me and I'll show you where she is.' Mr Hughes set off over the rough grass, two skinny Welsh collies at his ankles.

'Here, look see?' He pointed at the ground. 'The ditch is tucked under the gorse and she's lying at the bottom. I haven't touched her, other than her hand, to find out if she was warm.'

Ben ducked under spiky branches, trying to avoid needle-like leaves, Jack at his side. The young girl was dressed in bright, partygoing clothes, hair dyed a hot pink, silver stars stuck to her cheeks like frozen tears, and skin as pale as frost. She wore thick, black make-up, which was smudged around fixed, glassy eyes that stared sightlessly at the canopy of gorse. Ben felt her throat but couldn't find a pulse.

'Well, you're right, sir, she's dead. How did you come to find her?' he asked.

'Been here hours, I have, picking up rubbish. Four whole bags full of cans and bottles – and worse,' the elderly farmer grumbled. 'Bloody kids, not a thought for anyone else.' He stifled a sob. 'I spotted her pink hair, thought she was more rubbish.'

A noise on the lane caught the men's attention and they watched an ambulance arrive, a couple of patrol cars and a

4x4 Ben recognised as belonging to the local doctor, Howard Chalmers.

'I'll fetch the troops over, boss,' Jack said and hurried away.

Ben searched the teenager's pockets and tugged out a small plastic bag containing a couple of white pills.

He held the bag high to show Gareth. 'I'm sure these will be the problem. I can't see a mark on her, looks as though she just curled up and went to sleep.'

'That's what I thought when I first saw her,' Gareth mumbled, 'until I touched her hand – then I realised. Her poor parents, what a tragedy. Why don't people keep a better eye on their youngsters?'

Jack returned with the paramedics, DCs Mark Jefferies and Julie Smith – Jack's partner – and two uniformed officers, PC Ian Bradshaw and a recent recruit, PC James Spencer. The doctor and paramedics squeezed in under the bushes and before too long managed to extricate the body, strapping it to a stretcher ready for removal.

Another vehicle drew up in the lane and Ben recognised Stacey's old car. He walked up the slight incline to meet her.

'Hi, Pumpkin. What are you doing here?' he asked.

'Told you I'd be in the area. I was on my way home when I saw the cavalry heading out here, so U-turned and tagged on at the end. What's going on?'

'Mr Hughes found a body. Fairly safe to assume she was one of the partygoers.'

They moved closer to the group and Stacey stared at the girl's face before it was covered with a red blanket.

She gasped. 'I saw her the night of the dance, just before you lot arrived. She pushed past me with a young guy, boyfriend maybe.'

'Do you know who she is?' Jack asked.

'No, but I definitely recognise her. That pink hair is very distinctive.' Stacey wiped her eyes with the back of her hand. 'How sad she looks, like a broken butterfly.'

Ben searched the dead girl's pockets again but discovered nothing new.

'No identity on her,' he said. 'Someone is missing a daughter. Let's get back to the station and start work. Constable Bradshaw, I want you to take Spencer with you and follow the body to the morgue. Smith and Jefferies, we'll meet you back at base. Make a start on the missing persons list, will you. There's nothing more to do here.'

Chapter three

The next morning, Ben's phone rang as soon as he sat at his desk; he snatched up the receiver.

'DI James.'

'Morning, sir. Constable James Spencer here, Builth.'

'What have you got for me?' Ben asked.

'We may have discovered the identity of the dead girl. Mrs Mair Evans from the town rang first thing. Her daughter is overdue. Kid went away for a couple of days with her boyfriend, due back last night, but didn't show and her mobile is switched off. Mum says she's usually very good at keeping in touch and it isn't like her to go off radar.'

'What's her daughter's name?'

'Izzy Evans, seventeen. Fella is John Williams, lives in Llandrindod in one of the bail hostels.'

'Has Mrs Evans been able to contact him?'

'No, says she's tried, but no luck. I think that's why she's worried. The description she provided seems to match, young girl, pink hair…'

'Give me her address. We'd better make a house call.' Ben listened as Spencer read out the details, hung up and called for Jack, who appeared from the hallway.

'Yes, boss?'

'You busy with anything?'

Jack shook his head.

'Good. Seems we may know who our dead girl is. A worried mother has been in touch with Builth and we need to make a visit. Find a car, will you, and I'll meet you out front.'

* * *

Jack sped along the main road and they were soon parked outside a large house on the edge of the town. The front garden was well kept and a shiny, top-of-the-range BMW shared the wide drive with an elderly Ford Escort, bright red with pink flowers on the doors and across the boot. As they walked past the vehicles, Jack peered in through the windows of each. The BMW was immaculate, the Escort less so – empty takeaway packets were spread across the back seats and a row of fluffy animals perched on the parcel shelf.

'How can anyone see out the window through that menagerie?' Jack grumbled.

Ben rang the doorbell and heard it echo in the hall beyond. A minute passed before a smartly dressed, middle-aged woman flung the door wide open, worry and expectation on her face. A thick layer of make-up did nothing to mask her concern.

'Have you found her?' she asked, breathlessly.

'Mrs Mair Evans?' Ben asked.

The woman nodded.

'I'm DI James and this is DS Trent. Can we come in? Better than talking out here.'

She nodded again and stood to one side as the officers stepped into the hall.

'First left,' she said, 'we'll sit in the living room. Can I make you a cup of tea, gentlemen?'

'No thanks, Mrs Evans, we're OK.'

Jack walked past her and entered a large opulent room. Leather-bound books filled dark wooden shelves and several lighted display cabinets lined the end wall. Jack peered through the glass at a large collection of natural crystals and a few cut gemstones in every shape and colour imaginable. Plush, heavy curtains hung either side of a deep bay window and, squinting through leaded glass, he could just make out the river, sliding by an old landing stage at the bottom of the garden. The back garden was immaculate, like the front. The lawns were well kept: beds of roses and miniature conifers pockmarked the sweep of grass, packed borders lined the edges and a good-sized greenhouse was set off to one side. A mature horse chestnut spread its branches towards the water and sheltered a log cabin-like building; a summer house, he guessed.

'You have a beautiful home, Mrs Evans,' Jack said. 'The garden must be a lot of work.'

'I have help,' she said dismissively. 'Please, tell me about my daughter. Have you found her? I expect she's got herself into trouble again, that damn boy she's seeing is such a bad influence. Not that she listens to me.' She settled herself in a leather armchair and waved a hand in the direction of the sofa. The men sat facing her.

'Do you have a recent picture of your daughter?' Ben asked.

Mrs Evans stood and walked over to the large fireplace. She lifted down a silver frame and passed it to him.

'That's my Izzy. Taken a couple of months ago, before she ruined her hair. Why she has to be so wild I don't know. She was such a sweet girl before she met him.'

'Izzy's boyfriend?' Jack queried.

Mrs Evans nodded. 'He's led her astray before, dreadful influence. I've been trying to call him too, but he's not answering his phone.' She smoothed her skirt over her knees. 'So, where is she then?'

Ben cleared his throat. 'I'm sorry to have to tell you, Mrs Evans, but we think she was involved with the rave at Garth a couple of days ago.'

'Stupid girl! I told her John Williams would get her into trouble, but did she take any notice? Where is she? Locked up? That would probably do her good, make her realise actions have consequences. Do you need me to bail her out or something? Is that why you're here?' She turned an irritated gaze towards Jack who shifted uncomfortably in his seat.

'I'm very sorry, Mrs Evans,' Ben began, 'but we have found a body and have reason to believe it is your daughter, Izzy.'

Mrs Evans' hand flew to her mouth. 'Dead? Are you saying she's dead? That can't be right. That dreadful boy! He's involved in this, isn't he? Has that' – she searched for the word – 'toerag killed Izzy? How can she be dead? She's only seventeen for God's sake, she can't be.' Her face was white with shock, trembling hands fluttered over her mouth. 'No, no this can't be true. She wasn't anywhere near Garth, told me she was going to Rhayader, eighteenth birthday party for one of her friends. You must have the wrong girl, Inspector.'

Mrs Evans studied their faces and something seemed to shatter inside as she recognised the truth in their eyes. She crumpled and began to sob uncontrollably.

Jack moved to her side, placed a large, steadying hand on the heaving shoulders and spoke gently. 'Is there a Mr Evans?' he asked. 'We'll need to speak with him and you could do with company. Could you give me his number?'

Mrs Evans flapped her hand towards a telephone sitting on a highly polished occasional table near the door.

'In the address book, but he's away; Thailand – for work.' She sniffed and searched for a tissue in a large, designer handbag.

'What does your husband do?' Ben asked.

'He's a gem dealer. Not due back for another three weeks.' Taking a deep breath, she asked. 'Where is she? Where's my little girl? Can you take me to her? I must see her.'

'Of course.' Ben hauled himself out of the sofa. 'She's been taken to Brecon and we'll drive you over now if you'd like. Do you have anyone who can accompany you?'

'My neighbour might. Julia Henderson, number three.' Mrs Evans blew her nose and wiped her face, streaking black mascara across her cheeks.

Ben nodded at Jack, who left the room in search of the neighbour, while Mrs Evans repaired her face, put on her jacket and stumbled out to the car.

* * *

In the quietness of a side room, Jack gently removed the sheet covering the dead girl's face, her bright pink hair a shocking contrast against the starched, white cotton. Mrs Evans' hand flew to her mouth, but was unable to stop a howl of anguish escaping. Julia Henderson held her friend's arm, tried to guide her gently from the room, but the distraught mother pulled away from her grasp and collapsed on the bed, lying across her daughter's body, still howling. A technician rushed in to see what the noise was about and with persistence, managed to lead Mair Evans out of the viewing area and into a family room. The officers followed, shoulders slumped. No matter how many bereaved relatives he spoke to, Ben could never get used to the misery – he always felt as though he was being crushed.

After a few minutes, Mair calmed a little, the howling stopped and was replaced by a desperate, quiet sobbing. Mrs Henderson hugged her friend tightly, smoothing hair away from her face and trying to stem the flow of tears.

She glanced at Jack. 'Can you tell us what happened, Sergeant?'

'We think she took something,' he said. 'We are waiting for a toxicology report, but we found pills in her pocket.'

Mrs Evans struggled to her feet, face twisted with anger. 'Don't be so ridiculous, you stupid man!' she snapped. 'Izzy would never take drugs, that can't be why she died. Drugs indeed! You didn't know her, she was very anti-drugs, she'd never have done anything like this.'

'Please,' Ben implored, 'sit down, let's talk about this calmly. Izzy may have said she was against drugs, but most young people do – if you ask them – and it was a rave, there are always illegal substances at events like that.'

'It must have been that bloody boy, John Williams. I have no idea why Izzy wanted to hang around with him and his gang in town. We're a nice family, Inspector, nice people, we're not involved in anything like this, never have been. It's him you want. I bet he gave them to her. Nasty little sod. Did you know he lives in a bail hostel?'

Ben nodded.

'His place isn't far from here,' Mrs Evans continued. 'I demand you take me to his flat so we can get the truth out of him. How could he?' She started to moan and another breakdown seemed likely.

'We will call on him certainly,' Jack said, 'but it'll be best all round if you go home. Mrs Henderson, can you stay with your friend for a while? I'll arrange a car to take you both home when you are ready.'

The woman nodded. 'Of course.'

'Good. Thanks. We'll go and have a chat with John and call in to see you afterwards. Mair, go home and ring your husband, ask him to cut his trip short, I'm sure he'll want to be with you at this time and we'll talk again in a couple of hours.'

Mrs Evans slumped on the tatty sofa and stared at the cream wall opposite, tears running down her face; the second application of make-up smudged and lined. Ben and Jack left the room and while Ben consulted with the morgue staff, Jack brought the car round to the front entrance. They travelled in silence to Llandrindod Wells and Jack parked outside the main bail hostel.

Chapter four

John Williams lived on the top floor of an impressive, brick-built, Victorian town house, in the spa town of Llandrindod Wells. Many of the large houses on the road had been converted into flats and some – like this one – into hostels for the unemployed, those on bail, and those who may otherwise be on the streets.

As the officers approached the main door, it opened and a slight figure, in a grey hooded top pulled well over the eyes, slipped out. Jack shoved his hand in the rapidly narrowing gap as the door began to close and pushed it open, motioning for his boss to enter first. They climbed the staircase which grew narrower the higher they went. Ben guessed the top rooms of the once grand house were used to house servants – back in the day.

Jack banged on a cheap plywood door, paint scored and grubby, grease stains around the Yale lock. He heard no sound from the other side, so he banged again and kept on banging until eventually the door cracked open as far as the chain would allow.

A dishevelled youth peered out. He was a thin lad, of average height and build, his hair long, hanging down to his shoulders. He wore a baggy multicoloured vest and loose grey jogging bottoms, a white stripe on the side of each leg, a hand-rolled cigarette dangling from his mouth. Jack shoved a warrant card under the boy's nose and reluctantly he removed the chain.

'What do you want?' the lad asked, shuffling into the kitchen.

Ben opened his notebook. 'Are you John Williams?'

John nodded.

'Boyfriend of Izzy Evans from Builth, attended the rave near Garth at the weekend?'

Another cautious nod.

'Did you leave together?' Jack asked.

'Look, what's this all about?' John asked. 'I've only just got up, haven't had a cup of tea yet. You guys want one?'

'No thanks,' Ben said. 'We want you to tell us about the rave and what happened after it was stopped.'

John yawned and stretched. 'Can't remember much, to be honest with you. Danced most of the night and by the time you lot turned up, I was pretty wasted. I think I got a lift home with a mate, but couldn't really tell you who. It's all a bit fuzzy.' He smiled weakly.

'What happened to Izzy?' Ben asked.

'Came with me, I guess. To be truthful, I don't remember much about the second half of the night, I'd uh… drunk too much.'

Jack glared at him across the table. 'Drunk too much? Yeah right! You were out of your face, weren't you? What did you take, pills, coke? Give any to Izzy?'

The lad grew wary, shifted in his seat and studied the surface of the dirty table, picking at a dried spot of food with a grubby fingernail.

Jack was beginning to lose his patience. 'Come on, John, tell us what we want to know.'

'I still don't understand what this is all about,' John grumbled indignantly. 'You come here first thing in the morning, drag me out of bed and fire questions at me.'

‘Hardly first thing.’ Ben glanced at his watch. ‘It’s well after lunch. Look, you can talk to us here, or we’ll wait for you to get dressed and take you to the station, ask our questions there.’

John said nothing. Jack moved behind the lad, placed both of his large hands on John’s shoulders and bent to hiss loudly in his ear.

‘Izzy’s dead, you idiot. Found this morning in a bloody ditch and I haven’t got enough time to pussyfoot round this. I want to know what you’d been taking that night.’

‘Dead? No that can’t be right.’

‘I’m not making it up,’ Jack growled. ‘Tell us what you were taking.’

John lowered his head and shrugged his shoulders angrily. ‘Nothing much,’ he mumbled, ‘a couple of spliffs with an ecstasy chaser.’

‘Got any here?’ Jack asked.

‘No, took ’em all at the party.’

‘Did Izzy take some?’

‘Yes.’ John slumped in his chair. ‘Is she really dead or are you winding me up?’

‘I’m sorry.’ Ben shook his head. ‘Did she get the drugs from you?’

‘What? No! She brought the gear with her and gave some to me, not the other way round, so don’t try to nick me for supply. Izzy brought the pills, said they were new, stronger with a better come-down.’

‘How did you know they were ecstasy?’ Jack asked.

‘Cos she told me. Seemed like an E, stronger like she said, but they always vary a bit.’

‘Believe everything you’re told, do you?’ Jack snapped. ‘Come on, get dressed, we need to drive you to the station and take a statement.’

‘Aw, come on. Play fair. You said we could talk here and after all… my girlfriend has just died.’ John looked pleadingly at the large man towering over him.

'That was before you told us you'd been taking illegal drugs. Come on, we're not nicking you – yet. Just want a statement. We need to find out exactly what happened to Izzy for her parents' sake.'

* * *

Ben pulled up in the lane outside Jack and Julie's cottage in Llywel. Stacey led the way to the back garden and found Jack lighting candles in jam jars on the patio.

'Hey you two,' he called. 'Good to see you. Help yourselves to chairs from the outhouse.'

Ben dragged out four chairs as Julie appeared in the garden carrying a tray loaded with bowls of curry and a stack of naan bread.

'My favourite,' Stacey said. 'I adore your curries.'

Julie smiled at her. 'Glad you could make it. We haven't had a get together for ages, it seems.'

'It has been ages, we've all been so busy.' Stacey sat next to Ben and rested her hand on his thigh.

Jack dropped into a chair opposite and helped himself to a full bowl.

'How did you get on today with the Izzy business?' Stacey asked after few minutes.

Ben sighed. 'Pretty much as you'd expect. Her mum's in an awful state, Dad's away on business and the boyfriend doesn't seem bothered one way or the other, only really concerned in case we nick him for supplying the drugs. Selfish little git. John Williams told us Izzy had brought the drugs with her and gave some to him. I don't think we'll be able to prove it one way or the other, but I'm not convinced.'

'Could be that way round,' Jack mumbled around a mouthful of food. 'Williams lives on the top floor of a bail hostel and doesn't own much. No past convictions for anything drug related, seems he enjoys driving other people's cars away – without their permission – that and the odd shoplifting offence; no drugs though. I guess Izzy doesn't have a cash flow problem so maybe she did buy them.'

Ben said, 'Yeah, anything is possible, but I don't want to have to be the one to suggest it to her mother. Don't forget – they are "nice people".'

Stacey poured herself a second glass of wine. 'Such a waste, a young girl like that with everything to live for. Nice home, caring parents. John on the other hand… seems like no one cares for him, stuck in a hostel, no job and not much of a future. I can see why some kids turn to drugs, especially the poor ones. If you're off your face maybe the world seems bearable.'

'Not as simple as that, Stacey.' Jack chuckled. 'Come on, you're a woman of the world – journalist, no less – you know it doesn't work as neatly as that. The tabloid press is full of misdeeds of the "undeserving poor", the benefit cheats, the work shy with their fifteen children and flat-screen tellies, wild parties, drink and drugs. Sleeping around.' He drank from his glass before continuing. 'The upper classes are just the same, you know they are. Human nature isn't different because of how much money you have. The richer you are the better drugs you can buy, quality alcohol, not cheap cider from the corner shop, and their parties are bigger. A lot of them evade their taxes and pay for expensive advisors to help them do it – that's benefit cheating surely. And don't forget…'

'What?' Stacey asked.

'You haven't been able to buy a telly that hasn't got a flat screen for well over ten years.' He grinned victoriously at his audience.

Julie giggled. 'He can be a right working-class hero can Jack. Come on.' She pulled at his arm. 'Bed for you, *cariad,* it's late. Good job we're all on a late shift tomorrow.' She smiled at Stacey. 'The spare room is ready for you, see you at breakfast.'

Chapter five

The morning sun had already begun to heat up the day and the group decided to eat breakfast on the patio. Jack was in charge of the cooking, Ben lounged on one of the reclining chairs, while the women busied themselves laying the table and keeping coffee mugs filled. After an hour or so, Jack banged a tin tray with his wooden spoon.

'Come and get it,' he yelled from the kitchen.

They were soon sitting in front of heavily laden plates, covered in mounds of scrambled egg, grilled tomatoes, mushrooms, fried bread, and local bacon and sausages.

'There must be a whole pig here, Jack,' Ben exclaimed. 'Why do you always cook so much food?'

'Let's put it this way, boss,' Jack mumbled around a mouthful of food. 'The plates are always clean. Good job I haven't got a dog, I'd never have any leftovers to feed it.'

They fell silent, concentrating on their food. Flights of swallows were out in force swooping around the cottage catching insects, and a pair of house martins chittered loudly from a mud nest built under the eaves of the low building. At the end of the garden the mountain land rolled away and swooped over another peak. On the far side of the valley, sheep and their growing lambs grazed, resembling aspirin spilled on a green quilt.

Stacey took a sip of coffee and smiled at Jack. 'I love your breakfasts, matey. Don't listen to grumpy pants. He always sees a full plate as a challenge, thinks he has to clear the lot. I have the same problem at home.'

'Not my fault,' Ben grumbled. 'If I didn't eat everything on my plate when I was a nipper, dad used to whack me. Hard man, my dad, ex-miner, pensioned off when part of the mine fell on him, couldn't stand wasting anything. Don't know how Mum put up with him. I couldn't, left home as soon as I could. My brother ran away to Asia and so far hasn't come home.'

The conversation stalled and Jack cleared his throat a little awkwardly.

'Anyway… eat up. At least you won't need much later on.'

Stacey sighed and pushed her plate away. 'That's me done. All I want to do now is crawl back to bed and sleep it off. That's the most I've eaten in a week. When do you guys have to set off to the station?' she asked.

Ben checked his watch. 'About an hour. Do you have anywhere to be?'

Stacey nodded. 'Brecon. Sam wants me to pop in to cast an eye over the newbie reporter, Andrew Carr. Let's clear the dishes, Julie, and we can get on with our day.'

* * *

Ben collected a tray of coffee for his team, threaded his way through the incident room to his desk, settled himself and began sorting through mail. The second envelope he opened contained the autopsy and toxicology reports on Izzy Evans. Sipping scalding coffee, he began to read.

The report was detailed and conclusive. Izzy Evans had ingested a large quantity of methylenedioxymethamphetamine, otherwise known as MDMA. Tests on residues found in her body were able to show the drug was present in large amounts and had been adulterated with a cutting agent, identified as ketamine – a horse tranquilliser – together with traces of unidentified substances. The report included evidence of 'disseminated intravascular coagulation', together with an 'intracranial haemorrhage'. After a few minutes surfing the net, Ben was able to translate the medical terms into language he could understand. The pathologist had discovered blood clots in Izzy's small blood vessels and a haemorrhage inside her skull. Either condition could be lethal. Ben sighed and wondered for the thousandth time why young people took such risks with drugs. They really had no idea what they were swallowing. He turned back to the toxicology results, but soon felt swamped by chemical terms. The death certificate confirmed 'drug overdose' as cause of death. There was no doubt.

Ben called PC Bradshaw over. 'Ian, take a look at this for me, will you? Make sure I haven't missed anything. Scientific terms have never been my strong point, but I need to be sure what I'm talking about before I visit Mrs Evans again.'

'Sure, boss, no problem. When are you planning to go?'

'As soon as.'

'I'll get on with it then.'

DS Trent banged in through the door, his nose buried in a cardboard file.

'Jack. I've just received the autopsy and toxicology reports, Ian has them if you want a look. Izzy died from an ecstasy overdose. We ought to go and talk to Mair Evans, let her know.'

'Yeah, I'll come with you.' He flopped onto a nearby chair. 'I've been checking through John Williams' statement and can't see we can nick him for supply. We found pills on Izzy, nothing on him and no history with drugs either. I think he was telling the truth when he said she'd provided them.' Jack frowned. 'That's not going to go down well with her mum. I'll give her a call, make sure she's in later. May as well get it out of the way.'

* * *

Stacey made her way through reception at *The Mid Wales Times* offices, nodded at the young girl behind the desk, then trotted upstairs to her editor's office. The door was standing open, so she rapped with her knuckles and walked in.

'Hi, boss, how's tricks?' she asked.

Sam Jenkins, a large lumpy man, overfilled the leather chair behind his desk, forcing the arms outwards, and as he moved, the entire structure groaned and squeaked.

'Stacey.' He smiled. 'Fine, thanks.' He struggled to his feet. 'Excellent timing. I'd like you to meet our young newshound, Andrew Carr. Andrew, this is Stacey Logan. She can be a real pain in the arse sometimes, but knows what she's doing, you could learn a lot from her.'

An early twenty-something, dark-haired man stood and held out a hand towards Stacey, who shook it warmly.

'Nice to meet you,' they said in unison and laughed.

'That's what I like to see,' Sam said. 'Everybody happy and getting along, even though I'll have two of you fighting over the front page now. Stacey, did you read Andrew's court report?'

She nodded. 'I did. Good job! Won't take long for you to find your feet. Fresh out of Plymouth Uni, I understand.'

Andrew grinned. 'That's right. Ran the student newspaper there for a couple of years and wrote several freelance articles for the local press. I'm grateful for the chance to work on the staff of a proper paper.'

'I'm not sure "proper" is the correct description.' Stacey giggled. 'What assignments have you given him, boss?'

'He'll be covering the courts and the sports section, help him acclimatise if he covers a few local rugby matches.' He glared at his new staff member. 'Go on then, off you go. Stories don't get printed if they aren't reported and you can't report anything if you're sitting on your backside in here.'

Andrew leapt off his chair, gathered his belongings and made for the door. Stacey caught his eye; she raised an eyebrow and he hid a smile behind his spiral-bound notebook. She closed the door behind him and sat opposite Sam.

'How did you find him? He seems nice,' she said.

'Distant relative, something like a third-step-cousin-removed, on the wife's side. Gained a good degree though, wouldn't be here if he wasn't going to earn his keep. Speaking of which, have you got anything for me?'

'Update on the Izzy Evans story, overdose, very sad.' Stacey hesitated. 'I'm thinking of working on a feature, "Drugs and the Dance Scene", something along those lines. Raving was huge in the nineties, then the laws were changed and now outdoors dancing happens less often. Impromptu events like the one at Garth are becoming rarer. I'd like to discover how it works, who has the idea and chooses the venue. Do the organisers have anything to do with the drug supply? You know the sort of thing. Other than that, no, nothing new.'

'Any chance you can get an interview with Izzy's grieving parents? Maybe their experiences would be a timely warning to others.'

'I'm ahead of you, Sam. I have an appointment later in the week, gotta give them some space though.'

'OK, you work on that and I'll hand over the run-of-the-mill stuff to our new cub reporter. He needs the experience.' Sam opened a fat ring binder, flipped pages and Stacey guessed she was dismissed.

She left the offices of the newspaper and without anything pressing to do, wandered around the town centre. The streets were busy, gangs of tourists made the most of glorious weather, gift shops and restaurants were well populated. Stacey ambled from street to street, treated herself to a cup of coffee in the posh cafe near the antique centre and managed to resist a plate of Welsh cakes. It wasn't as though she was hungry after her huge breakfast. Strolling into the covered market, she brought some provisions for her store cupboards, including a large chunk of Purl Wen, a Welsh blue cheese. Pausing at the long noticeboard in the entrance, she gazed at the many cards pinned there. Jewellers and knife sharpeners advertised their services, and there were plenty of second-hand cars and prams for sale, litters of working dogs, notices for concerts, craft fayres and markets. A bright orange piece of A5-sized card caught her attention and she read an advert for an upcoming dance event in the grounds of a large country house not far from town. She scribbled down the details in her notebook, before heading to the car park.

* * *

Ben and Jack returned to the office hot, irritable and badly in need of coffee. The sun had been beating down all day and on the way back from Builth Wells, they became embroiled in a long traffic jam on the main road, caused by an overturned caravan.

The earlier interview with Mrs Evans had been extremely difficult. The bereaved mother refused to accept her daughter had either supplied drugs, or taken any voluntarily. She insisted John Williams must have slipped them into Izzy's drink. While they were at the house, Izzy's father, Robert Evans, arrived home from Thailand, pale beneath his tan, jet-lagged and distressed. Emotions were stretched as tightly as the strings on a Welsh harp and at one point, Mair Evans demanded John be arrested and charged with murder. The home visit had not been easy.

PC Bradshaw glanced up as they walked in. 'How'd it go?'

'Not great,' Jack muttered, 'but these things rarely do.'

'I've been checking a few things while you've been out,' Ian said.

'Oh yes?' Jack was interested. '

'Well, I've been looking at the tox report and the analysis of the pills found on Izzy, then had a bit of a hunt online. This business of cutting MDMA with ketamine, well, it's not that common as ketamine is a party drug in its own right; it does happen though and seems to be occurring more often locally. I've discovered two cases in Bridgend, three in Swansea and a couple more in Cardiff. The chemical make-up of all the ecstasy involved is identical. Therefore–'

Ben butted in, 'They all come from the same batch.'

'Exactly! Not only are they all the same, but they've appeared on the scene fairly recently, so maybe we have a new source out there.'

'Haven't heard about anyone new on the streets,' Jack said. 'I know most of the dealers around town and none of my snitches have said anything.'

'The pills we found on Izzy had "5c" – like five cents – stamped on one side, a star on the other, same as the ones recovered in those recent cases. I reckon there is a new kid on the block,' Ian said.

Jack nodded. 'With such a widespread area of distribution, it could be a large organisation,' he said. 'How can we track them down, I wonder? Got any photos of the pills, Constable?'

Ian shuffled through pages in the file, slipped out a black-and-white shot and handed it to Jack who examined the photo carefully.

'Nope, haven't seen anything like these,' he said, 'but I'll keep my eyes open. Run off a few copies, will you, and I'll pass them round the stations, make sure the foot soldiers know what to look for. Let's see if we can discover how far these things have spread, and who knows, we might get lucky and catch a dealer who will spill the beans.'

'Good work, Ian,' Ben said. 'Keep at it, see if you can uncover any other incidents. Anything you find, pass it on to DS Trent, he could do with a project.'

Chapter six

Stacey pulled into the drive of a large house on the outskirts of Builth Wells, parked behind a red Escort and climbed out of her car. She saw the front curtain in the bay window twitch, so was not surprised when the door was opened before she'd walked up the path.

A middle-aged man stood on the step. He was dressed in smart, casual clothes, maybe early forties, hair beginning to recede, and had a healthy tan, but that was as far as it went. His eyes drooped at the corners and matched his downward turned mouth, shoulders slumped, as though he bore a heavy weight on his back.

'Ms Logan?' he called. 'Please, come in. Robert Evans.' He held out a hand and Stacey shook it before following him into the wide hallway.

'Come and wait in the living room,' Robert said. 'I'll give Mair a shout, she's been lying down. Not dealing with this very well, to be honest, neither of us are. You never expect to lose your child, that's not the way things should be.'

Robert ushered Stacey into the large front room and called his wife from the bottom of the stairs.

'Mair! Mair, love. Stacey Logan from *The Mid Wales Times* is here. I'll put the kettle on and make some coffee.'

Stacey listened as the man moved further into the house and heard a kettle being filled. A few moments passed and Mair Evans shuffled into the room. Stacey stood to greet her. The older woman looked exhausted, black rings beneath badly swollen eyes, no make-up, hair tousled from the pillow.

She smiled weakly. 'Nice to meet you, Ms Logan, thank you for coming.'

'No, thank you for allowing me to visit at this difficult time. I am truly sorry for your loss. How are you, Mrs Evans?'

Mair shrugged her shoulders.

'Surviving, but only just. I keep thinking I hear my daughter upstairs and have to check her room to convince myself she's not there.' She sniffed. 'Izzy spent most of her day in her room, doing whatever it is teenagers do, so I didn't see that much of her. We didn't do family meals when her father was away working. Now she's not here though, I miss her desperately.' Tears slid from already red eyes.

Mr Evans bumped the door with a tea tray and placed it on a low coffee table in front of his wife. He reached over, squeezed one of her hands and smiled encouragingly before handing round mugs.

Stacey thanked him then said, 'So, what can I do to help you? You called the paper's offices and spoke to Sam Jenkins, the editor.'

Mair nodded. 'We want to do something to stop this happening to other parents. I had no idea Izzy was into anything like this, drugs I mean. True she'd occasionally come home the worse for wear from having drunk too much, but I never even considered she was taking drugs. When we'd talked about them, she always said she wasn't interested. Maybe if I had known what to look for, the signs, I might have been able to prevent this from happening. I feel as though I've somehow failed as a mother.' She buried her face in a lace handkerchief, tears falling thickly.

'Don't be daft, love.' Mr Evans put an arm across his wife's shoulders. 'You have always been a great mother. Izzy didn't want for anything, you know that. Come on now, hush. You've cried enough, we have to move on.' He turned to Stacey. 'We want to set up a charity, "The Izzy Evans Trust", to help other families who have suffered similar tragedies and maybe, if we can increase awareness of the dangers, we might prevent others having to go through it. Does that make sense?' he asked.

'Perfectly,' Stacey said. 'It's a wonderful idea and I'll do all I can to publicise it.'

'Izzy had a trust fund, to help with her education,' Robert said. 'I started paying into it when she was born and as my business took off, I was able to stash away a sizable amount.' He sighed, eyes full of sorrow. 'She won't need it now, will she? We'll use the cash to get things moving.'

Stacey took out a spiral-bound pad and began to scribble notes.

'My editor said you are a gem dealer, Robert, that's interesting,' she said. 'Sounds very exotic, what exactly do you do?'

'Just that really, buy and sell cut stones. I've always been interested in geology, earned a first at Bristol University and wondered what I could use it for. On a gap year, I travelled to Asia, stumbled across the gem dealers in Bangkok and was instantly hooked, quite good at it too, didn't get conned very often.'

Stacey scribbled notes as he related his tale.

'I broadened my horizons and found my way to Burma – Myanmar as it is now. While trekking high in the mountains, I discovered a tiny, family-run mine – pigeon blood rubies, beautiful. I returned four years running and the visits paid off. A large, flawless stone had been found and as a good customer, and friend of the family, I was given first refusal.' He smiled, the memories pleasant and warm. 'I made enough on that single stone to pay for all this and up my game. I buy bigger, better stones now, mostly to order and have travelled all over the world. I do enjoy Bangkok though, fascinating place. That's where I was when I heard…' he ran out of words.

Mair cleared her throat. 'So you really think this is a good idea, Ms Logan, to set up a trust? I'll need something to keep me busy.'

'I think it's a great idea and promise I'll do all I can to help. We'll rough out an article now, so tell me about Izzy, her life, interests and achievements, a recent photograph would be lovely, then we'll talk about the trust.'

'Thank you,' Robert muttered. 'We thought this would be a good way to keep her memory alive.'

Chapter seven

At four thirty in the morning, every available local officer and some from further afield were crammed into a room at Builth Wells police station. Excitement and anticipation crackled in the tense atmosphere as the force readied itself for an early morning raid. DS Trent's hard work had finally paid off and he had received some useful information from his snitches in the area.

There had been whispers of a hidden laboratory churning out illegal substances, ecstasy in particular, and they readily passed on the information. Jack had managed to obtain more samples of pills bearing the 5c and star marks, and his informant had pointed him in the direction of an empty house in one of the many outlying settlements on the edge of the military ranges.

Officers waited in the cramped and stuffy room, adjusting stab-proof vests, checking their kit, chatting, laughing, anxious to be off. Stacey Logan stood on one side feeling like a spare part, this wasn't the world she was used to. Sam Jenkins had somehow managed to arrange for her to tag along as an observer for the press and, never having attended anything like this before, she was especially nervous. Jack sidled up and stood by her side, watching the preparations intently.

'You OK?' he asked quietly.

'I think so. Exciting, isn't it?'

'A dawn raid certainly gets the blood pumping. Ben is going to pair you up with Mark Jefferies, keep you out of harm's way until we're inside and can secure the building. You never know what to expect in a situation like this. My source says it's a one-man operation, but that one man could be armed and prepared to protect his enterprise.'

Stacey smiled at her friend. 'I hope you'll be careful, Jack, we don't want you getting shot again.'

He chuckled. 'Neither do I, but I don't think that'll happen. The most important thing is you do exactly as you're told, when you're told to do it. DCI Ambrose is very twitchy about having you involved, but can see the benefit of Joe Public having a better idea of what we do. That's why you're here, very privileged.' He caught Ben's eye and nodded. 'Looks like we're off. Stick with Mark, I don't want Ben on my back if you come to any harm.' He looked her in the eye. 'I mean it, Stace, do as you're told. See you later.'

He pushed his way through the huddle of officers to stand at his inspector's side as last-minute instructions were issued.

The team left the room *en masse* and squashed into three transit vans. Jack and Ben rode in an unmarked car, Mark and Stacey in the back seat. The roads were empty and the small convoy covered the distance in good time. Within half an hour they halted at the end of a narrow lane leading to the settlement close to MoD land. According to Jack's information, an empty house on the edge of the hamlet was being used to manufacture pills bearing identical markings as those Dyfed Powys Police had already confiscated. The drivers turned off their headlights and crept slowly towards the target, anxious not to give the game away. The element of surprise in situations like this was what made any raid successful. They didn't want to blow it now.

The teams climbed out of vans and assembled in front of an ordinary, run-down, three-bedroom semi. According to council records, the place hadn't been occupied for six years or more, becoming shabbier as time passed and nature reclaimed the building. The garden was an overgrown tangle with meadow-length grass; dense banks of nettles and thistles, and brambles had buried fences under thick leafy briars. A moss-stained 'for sale' notice was nailed to the wood cladding next to the front door and another sprouted from a post in the front garden.

A heavily built constable from Llandrindod crept up the path towards the door, a metal battering ram in his arms. The rest of the squad followed, half a dozen split away from the main group and silently made their way to the rear of the property.

Ben waited until he was sure everyone was in place. His eyes swept across his squad and received nods and thumbs up from all. They were ready. He glanced quickly towards the road and spotted Stacey waiting with DC Mark Jefferies. She caught him looking and smiled, holding a thumb in the air to signal things were fine. Ben turned back and signalled to the guy with the battering ram. Time seemed to stand still for a couple of seconds before the officer grasped the metal handles, swung the heavy lump away from the door, then back again with a mighty whack. The door frame shattered as though made of glass and the door flew open. The impact was deafening after the silent approach and Stacey jumped. Mark placed a warning hand on her arm and she watched intently.

As soon as the door was open, the first wave of police surged into the hallway. There was a loud crack from the back of the house as a second door was smashed open and more officers flooded in. Ben and Jack were close behind and watched as two of their men ran up the stairs, the rest quickly and efficiently checking the downstairs rooms.

Shouts of 'Clear!' filled the house, then one of 'Sir! Front bedroom.'

Jack was closest to the stairs and galloped up, taking three at a time, Ben close behind. Two uniforms from Builth stood in the doorway of a bedroom and parted when Jack arrived behind them. Ben stepped into the dark room and saw someone cowering on the bed. A young man, early twenties, dressed in T-shirt and boxers, scrunched himself into the corner next to his bed, hands raised in front of his face as if to warn off blows.

He was terrified and yelled, 'Don't shoot! Don't shoot!'

'Constable Spencer,' Ben ordered, 'get him cuffed and you' – he addressed the screaming man on the bed – 'shut up, for God's sake! I can't hear myself think.'

Jack dragged open raggedy curtains and let the dawn light in. The room was a mess. In one corner a camping gas stove rested on an old table covered with dirty plates and cups. Half-eaten food spilled from open packets and a bin liner was propped up underneath the table, its contents bursting out. As well as the bed, there was a tatty looking armchair placed in front of a packing case on which sat a portable television. Clothes, books and magazines covered most of the floor, apart from two narrow tracks, one leading to the cooker, the other to the armchair.

'Sergeant, get downstairs and check with the teams, see what they've found,' Ben instructed and perched on the arm of the easy chair to face his prisoner. 'Now then, boy. What have you got to tell me?'

'What's going on?' the lad mumbled. 'What's happening? What are you doing here?'

'More to the point,' Ben said. 'What are you doing here?'

'I live here.'

'What's your name? We can find out, but this will be over quicker if you answer my questions – honestly, mind you.'

'Jeremy Cavendish.'

'Good. Now we're getting somewhere. So, Jeremy Cavendish, do you have permission to live here?'

'Not really, no. I'm squatting, that's all, just squatting.' Jeremy glanced up fearfully as DS Trent appeared in the doorway, his bulk nearly filling the door frame.

'There's a cook shop in the back room, boss, and plenty of these.' Jack held out a plastic bag and Ben took it, holding it up to the light. About a dozen small, white pills rattled around in the bottom. On closer inspection he saw they all bore the star and 5c marks.

Ben grinned. 'Well done, Sergeant. Read Jeremy his rights and send him to the station. I'll oversee the search, no idea how long this will take, oh, and you can inform our tame reporter she can come in, but make sure she stays with Mark and keeps out of the way.'

Jack dragged the wriggling youth downstairs and into the garden. Cavendish was shoved in the back of a waiting van and driven away. Jack signalled Stacey with his index finger and she walked over quickly, shadowed by DC Jefferies.

'DI James says you can go inside now, but don't get in the way and don't forget to follow instructions. You're allowed to take pictures, but we'll need to vet them before you can print any. At least I know you'll play fair. Not bad this, having a house-trained journalist,' Jack said with a chuckle.

Mark led the way along the path to the door and Stacey followed, camera in her hand. She was greeted by organised chaos. Uniformed officers worked busily in every room, searching everywhere. Floorboards were levered up so the space beneath could be checked, skirting boards removed for the same reason. In a smaller back room, which might be classed as a utility room, a mass of laboratory style equipment had been set up and on a side table was a mound of small bags filled with what appeared to be more ecstasy tablets. Officers were slowly and carefully dismantling the equipment and loading it into evidence boxes and large, sealable plastic bags, conscientiously completing the labels. Ben oversaw the operation watching everything. PC James Spencer was busy emptying an old metal filing cabinet of paperwork and stacking it in a box, while PC Ian Bradshaw was unplugging computer equipment. Stacey was fascinated by the activity and almost forgot to use her camera. The atmosphere felt like Christmas morning, everyone rushing to open their gifts, but in reverse – repacking them.

There was a shout from the front living room and Ben headed that way. The stout officer who had wielded the battering ram so effectively, had discovered a stash of completed product, Tupperware boxes crammed with pills. Ben examined them and saw they bore the distinctive markings. He began to smile and it rushed across his face, a proper Cheshire cat grin.

'Jack!' he called. 'We've hit the jackpot, come and take a look.'

All officers in earshot made for the living room creating a human jam in the doorway as they strained to see what had been found. Jack pushed and barged his way through and when he spotted the boxes spread out on the floor next to a hole in the boards, he grinned.

'Bingo!' he exclaimed and thumped his boss on the back. 'Now the real work starts. The scally we arrested will have been employed by someone, no way is this a one-man operation. He'll tell us who that someone is and we'll have a result. Don't know about you, boss, but I bloody love it when it all comes together. Right, I'm off to the station. I'm looking forward to a chat with Jeremy.'

Ben found Stacey and called her out of the house. 'Did you enjoy that?'

'God, yes, what a buzz,' she said. 'Just like you see on the telly, isn't it? I felt as though I was a part of a SWAT team. Sam will love this and I have most of the day to work on it. Thank you so much for helping to arrange this.'

'Don't forget to email me a copy before you send anything to that boss of yours, pictures too. I promise I'll check everything over as soon as it comes in and give you the thumbs up. Best if you get off now, though, the rest will be boring.' He glanced round at Mark. 'Take Stacey home, will you? Once you've dropped her off, get yourself to Builth. We're going to be working out of the large meeting room at the back, it's a better base than Llandovery. I'll catch up with you there. Jack was right, this is the beginning of the investigation – not the end.'

Chapter eight

The windowless interview room in the bowels of the Builth police station was stuffy and smelt of disinfectant and body odour. An electric fan whirred on a table in the corner and sounded like a wasp with a silencer fitted, but achieved little, merely moving hot air around and doing nothing to lower the temperature.

Ben and Jack sat on one side of a metal table, Jeremy Cavendish on the other. Mark leaned on the tiled wall at the back of the room. The recording machine whirred quietly and Ben was gathering his thoughts. He regarded the man opposite from underneath furrowed brows and Cavendish shifted uncomfortably in his chair.

'Right then, Jeremy,' Ben said, 'let's make a start. You understand why you're here, don't you?'

The prisoner stared at the tabletop and said nothing. He picked at a hang nail on his thumb, wincing when the skin finally came away and he sucked at the drop of blood.

Ben continued. 'OK, so let me spell it out for you. You have been arrested under suspicion of the manufacture and supply of class A drugs. We've collected more than enough evidence to put you away for a long time, so you don't really have to say anything at all if you don't want to.

We've got everything we need.' Ben paused. 'Thing is, Jeremy, we don't think you were working on your own and if you can help us by providing useful information leading to further arrests, we can help you, possibly reduce the very long sentence you are currently looking at.'

'Are you offering me a deal?' Cavendish asked.

'Depends on what you're offering us,' Jack said. 'You may as well give up your buddies, after all, why should you do their time as well as yours? That's what will happen if you refuse to talk to us.'

'I'd like to help, really I would, but I don't know who he is.'

'Don't be so stupid,' Jack growled. 'How do you expect us to believe that? Everyone in your position says the same thing and everyone is lying. Who is "he"?'

'I've never met him, honestly I haven't.' Cavendish rubbed his face. 'We communicated over the net, so it could have been anyone. May not even be a he.'

Ben asked, 'How did you two connect then? I can't see anyone posting an advert asking for someone to manufacture drugs.'

'Oh God,' the lad groaned. 'I got an email out of the blue. I'd finished at uni and was looking for a job, a lab job, technician or something, maybe research. Sent my CV out all over the place, hundreds of copies. Didn't get a reply from most, but every now and again I'd be called for an interview, then I got offered this… job.' He stopped talking and Ben waited, knowing Cavendish would feel compelled to fill the silence.

The young man sighed. 'I wouldn't need to know who I was talking to, would I?'

'Weren't you curious?' Jack asked.

'Not really, I needed a job and soon after the email, our conversations moved to the dark web. Governments haven't come close to breaking the encryption codes yet, so pretty much anything goes.'

'What happened next?'

'This whoever began by offering me a position as a research assistant at a small private lab in Mid Wales. We chatted online for a few weeks, then the conversations changed and gradually it became clear what this person wanted me to do. I wasn't overly keen, to be honest, but he promised to pay me in Bitcoins, you know the digital currency, and told me I was completely safe as it was a small organisation. I was to be the only chemist.'

'So you jumped in up to your neck, didn't you?' Jack asked.

'No, I didn't,' Cavendish protested. 'I thought about it for a long time but needed the money, man. Three years studying and I've been left with no job and a bloody enormous debt. I thought if I just made a couple of batches that would be enough to set me on the right track. I wasn't going to do it forever. Anyway, it was only Es. Everybody takes Es; not like smack, is it?'

Jack lost his temper and slapped the tabletop open-handed, the sound racketed round the room. Cavendish left his seat by a good six inches, eyes wide open, face shocked white.

'Listen to me.' Jack spoke in an angry hiss. 'A couple of weeks ago we found a seventeen-year-old girl with some of your filthy pills in her pocket. We couldn't ask her where she got them from because she was dead. You hear that? She was dead and yes – you've probably guessed it – your filthy pills killed her. We can do you for a lot worse than manufacture and supply of class As.'

Cavendish stared at him, slack jawed.

Jack continued. 'Now, DC Jefferies is going to take you back to your cell. The custody sergeant will bring you some lunch and while you eat, I want you to think carefully about the future, yours in particular. You are in so bloody deep it'll be years before you'll be able to climb out. How old are you now?' Jack checked his notes. 'Twenty-three, good age, I remember being twenty-three. You could get twenty years for this, maybe more. When you're released, you'll be well into middle age and back on the streets with jack shit, so think about that.'

Jack slapped off the recording equipment and Cavendish was returned to the cells.

* * *

Stacey was working on her feature about the dance scene in her small office and was startled when Ben appeared in the doorway.

'Hi, you,' he said.

'Blimey, you nearly gave me a heart attack, I didn't know you were coming, thought you'd be too busy processing everything you confiscated during the raid.'

He moved closer, wrapped a long arm around her body and peered at the computer screen.

'I was passing and thought I'd nip in while I had the chance. You're right, we'll be busy for a while but have a bit of a natural lull.' He leaned closer to the desk. 'Is this your article about the raid this morning?'

Stacey chuckled. 'No, that was sent to Sam as soon as you gave me the OK. It'll be on the front page tomorrow. Sam was very impressed and, with your help, I've earned a bucket load of brownie points, so thanks again for getting me involved.'

'No problem, glad I could talk Charlie Ambrose round. As you know he wasn't keen on the idea but I got there in the end.' He glanced at the screen again. 'So, what's this?'

'A feature I'm working on, "Drugs and the Dance Culture" – working title obviously, much more research required, so like you, I'm going to be busy too. Got time for a cuppa?'

'Definitely, thanks.'

Stacey shut down the computer, squeezed past her partner and went to the kitchen to put the kettle on. Ben followed and sat at the table as Stacey rounded up mugs and a large cafetiere.

'How are you getting on with the guy you nicked this morning?' she asked.

Ben sighed heavily. 'I think "slowly" best describes the situation.'

'Has he given you any names or is it a one-man operation?'

'He's confirmed he was working for someone else but says all contact with the boss was online so he doesn't have a name to give us.'

'Is he telling the truth?' Stacey plonked two mugs of coffee on the table and sat opposite her partner.

Ben groaned. 'I really don't know, but guess it's possible. One of the lads on our team is a whizz with computers so I'm hoping he'll discover something useful on the kit we seized.' He drank deeply and smiled. 'Aren't you tired after the early start?'

Stacey grinned. 'A bit, planning an early night – fancy joining me?'

'I was hoping for an invite, especially as I might not have much time off in the near future.'

'You know you're always welcome, that's why I gave you a key. How about you nip down to Llanwrtyd and pick up some fish and chips from the Neuadd Arms? No cooking or washing up, save my energy for later.' She giggled and Ben joined in.

'Marvellous idea. Warm up the plates, Pumpkin, I'm on my way.'

* * *

At nine in the morning, Jeremy Cavendish was once again huddled behind the metal-topped table in the interview room at Builth station, this time accompanied by a solicitor, Steve Bowen from a firm in Cardiff. He was an old-school lawyer in his sixties, smartly dressed with greying hair and a business-like, efficient manner. Definitely not a duty solicitor. Introductions had been made, the recording machine set up, and the interview began. DS Trent took the lead.

'I hope you slept well, Jeremy.' Jack didn't wait for an answer before continuing. 'At least you've had time to think about the mess you're in, and get yourself a brief, I see.' Jack nodded towards Bowen and said, 'I trust you have been able to consult with your client, sir?'

'Yes, thank you, Sergeant, for the time being.' Bowen opened a yellow legal pad and placed it on the table in front of him, a chunky fountain pen at the ready.

'Righto,' Jack said. 'Let's get to it then, Jeremy. During your interview yesterday, you told us you have never met the individual who paid you to cook up drugs for him. Is that right?'

Jeremy nodded.

'Speak up,' Jack ordered. 'The machine can't record nods.'

'No, I've never met him – or her, could be a her. I really haven't any idea who this person is.'

'How did this person introduce themselves? Did they give you a name?'

'They called themself, "The Colonel", like in the army, but everyone has nicknames on the net, no one uses their real name.'

'How long have you been in contact with this colonel? When did you team up?'

'I dunno, about six months ago maybe? Then a couple of months later I was told where I'd be working. It was obviously very covert. Even though we used the dark web, you can never be a hundred per cent sure someone isn't able to get in, see what you're up to. We had a code we used between ourselves, that's how he told me where the house was. He said that if I agreed to work for him, the lab would be set up and ready to go when I arrived. I had a few loose ends to tie up at home and came out here about ten weeks ago.'

Jack pondered for a moment, then asked, 'So, that's how it was? You arrived at the house and everything was set up?'

'Yep. Just like that. Plenty of food as well as chemical supplies, gas for the stove, even the telly was there. I was surprised the electricity and water were working. The place smelt bad with damp, didn't seem like it had been lived in for ages, but it did me. After all, I was only going to be there long enough to make a couple of batches and you can put up with anything for short periods of time.'

Jack grinned, he couldn't help himself. Jeremy Cavendish was more than likely going to have to learn how to put up with bad things for *long* periods of time.

The prisoner spotted the grin. 'What's so bloody funny? Play fair. You said if I helped you, you'd help me and I'm being as co-operative as I can, but I can't tell you what I don't know. I needed the money, this was a short-term fix, but…'

'But what, Jeremy?' Jack asked.

'Well, it all worked OK. I guess it was so easy that I didn't have a problem making up a few more batches. I was getting paid in Bitcoins, just like the colonel said, and I enjoyed the peace and quiet. I've always liked my own company and had nowhere else to be. There was so much food and other supplies in the house I didn't need to go out, so I worked, churning out pills. Watched the telly in the evenings and just chilled out, knowing all the time I was getting richer instead of poorer. Quite a culture shock after the last few years, I can tell you.'

'So for the best part of three months, you've been living by yourself in the house, making ecstasy tablets and stashing them under the floorboards, and in all that time, you didn't see or speak to anyone, not even the guy who recruited you?' Jack was incredulous. 'Didn't anyone ever come to pick up any of the finished product? I mean, they were paying you and the pills under the floorboards weren't going to sell where they were.'

'Twice I got a message via the net, asking me to pack up a box and hide it in the brambles by the back fence. The messages came in late at night. I was told to leave the pills outside, not to look out of the windows, and go to bed, and that's what I did. I felt like a spy and it made total sense. In the movies people don't know each other so if one gets caught they can't pull the others down with them.'

Ben sighed heavily. 'That's the problem, though, isn't it, Jeremy? You're telling us you don't know your puppet master, but you could be lying, trying to save your own skin. You're not being very helpful, are you?'

The young lad smiled weakly. 'I can be though, Inspector, if you're really prepared to offer a deal.' Cavendish and his solicitor watched the policeman intently and Ben guessed Steven Bowen knew what was about to be said.

'Until we know what you're offering, it's difficult,' Ben said, 'but if you can provide us with significant new information which will enable us to make other arrests, your cooperation will be taken into account at any future sentencing hearing. Your solicitor will have told you we can't make actual deals. That's the best we can do, but I will put a word in for you if you turn out to be useful.'

'Well–' the lad hesitated and glanced at his lawyer who gave a brief nod. 'I'm supposed to leave out a batch tonight, in the usual place. The gear you found under the floorboards was ready for collection. I could tell you where to leave the stuff, then you can watch until it is collected and nick whoever turns up.' He grinned. 'Is that info useful enough?'

* * *

Cavendish sat in his cell staring at the metal door. It was evening and he was fed up after spending so long locked up. The observation flap had been left open and from where he was perched on the stone bunk, he could see a small square of corridor, pale yellow paint under harsh fluorescent lights. He'd read all the graffiti scrawled on the walls several times over and even managed a couple of hours' fitful sleep on the thin, plastic covered mattress. He wondered if the coppers were at the house already, staking the place out to see who would come to make the collection. He wished they'd get on with it, though, he was fed up with the inside of the tiny cell. Steve Bowen had told him that if the operation went well, he may get bail, especially as he'd provided the information in the first place. Cavendish was pleased with his lawyer, he seemed to know what he was doing and had worked for his auntie for years. Thank God she'd agreed to pay the bill, he'd already worked out his Bitcoin stash would be confiscated.

He wished he had a watch. He had no real idea how long he'd been banged up and his phone had obviously been taken. He wondered whether they'd have taken his watch if he wore one. It was disorientating not knowing what the time was and how it was passing, especially after all the years he'd spent trying to beat the clock at university. He'd never seemed to have enough time for anything in the past and now had so much, he didn't know what to do with it. Maybe he should try to meditate or something. The beginnings of a nasty headache crept around inside his skull and when the custody sergeant had last checked on him, Jeremy had asked for some aspirin. Geraint Jones promised to bring some with supper.

What seemed like hours later, keys rattled in the corridor and the door swung open. A uniformed officer entered with the custody sergeant and carried a tray with a plate of what looked like stew, two slices of white buttered bread, a mug of tea, plastic utensils and two painkillers. After checking things were OK with their prisoner, they placed the food on the bunk next to him and left, shutting and locking the door behind them. This time the flap was snapped shut and Cavendish instantly experienced a touch of claustrophobia. He swallowed the pills and started on the food. Even though he didn't have much of an appetite, he had to admit the meal wasn't bad.

Chapter nine

The dark early morning was certainly cool, but luckily frost free, and Ben and Jack were sheltered from the stiff breeze. They were hunkered down in an ancient sheepfold on a rise overlooking the short row of semis on the edge of the ranges settlement. From there they had an excellent view of the building and garden, as well as the lane in and out, and the forestry tracks cutting through the mountains. Well dressed for the long wait they had arrived just after dark the previous evening, anxious no one should see their approach and give the game away. Confident they'd been successful, they crouched behind the crumbling wall and took it in turns to keep watch through a pair of night-vision binoculars set up on a tripod, the lenses just clearing the top of the stonework.

Ben rubbed his hands vigorously, tucking them under his armpits and burrowed deeper into his thick scarf.

'When do you think they'll come?' he asked.

'Could be any time, boss,' Jack answered. 'Some people say four o'clock in the morning is the best time to carry out anything like this, something to do with body rhythms – four in the morning is down time for the brain apparently, humans are less alert then. Perfect time to burgle a house with the occupants asleep upstairs, or launch any kind of an attack. No one's expecting it and everyone is more than half asleep. So, maybe around four, but I couldn't really tell you.'

'Nothing's moved on the roads for a couple of hours now,' Ben said, sounding worried, 'and I haven't heard anything from the lads in the cars. Hope they haven't been spotted.'

'They won't have been. Anyway, no one looks twice at tatty Land Rovers round here, it's not like we're using squad cars. We checked on the way in and they were a long way up the tracks. As soon as the light went, they became invisible. Be patient, boss. We don't even know if whoever is coming will use the road. They could walk in across country, use a scrambler bike, horse, bloody anything. We'll see them from up here, though. Come on, budge over and take the watch, I'm going cross-eyed and need a cup of coffee to keep me awake.'

The men shuffled about and Jack was soon lying with his back against the wall sipping from a plastic mug. Ben peered through the binoculars, full of expectant excitement. It would be brilliant if this paid off and they went back to the station with a prisoner. Maybe they'd even get to meet the colonel that Cavendish kept on about.

* * *

Sergeant Jones clocked on at six, ready to face the new day. There was only one prisoner in the cells and he wasn't much of a nuisance; well-behaved lad really, apart from running a cookhouse manufacturing illicit drugs. Cavendish was due in court this morning and would most likely be remanded, and Geraint wanted to ensure his charge had been fed and watered and offered a shower. He'd been a custody sergeant for years, always ran his cells by the book and couldn't abide corner cutting. He had an exemplary record that he had no wish to spoil as he was only a few months away from retirement.

He walked down to the cells with a mug of tea and a plate of buttered toast, unlocked the cell and discovered Cavendish still asleep on the thin mattress. The lad was curled up, knees under his chin, a thin, standard issue blanket thrown over his skinny body.

Sgt Jones put the tray down and called, 'Wakey, wakey, son. Cuppa and some toast here for you. Rise and shine.'

Cavendish didn't move, so the sergeant moved closer and gently shook the lad's shoulder. A thin arm slipped out from beneath the blanket and dangled at a stupid angle away from the raised bunk area, bounced, then was still. Geraint shook harder, leaning over to peer at his charge's face and finally it dawned on him that something was dreadfully wrong. He made for the cell door and hit the panic button on the wall outside. A discordant racket echoed in the corridor for a couple of seconds before he heard a mass of running feet as other officers in the station galloped down to the cells.

Mark Jefferies was the first to arrive, followed by James Spencer and a handful of other uniforms.

'What's up, Sarge?' Mark asked, dashing into the cell.

'Get the Doc quick, will you? The prisoner isn't breathing and he feels cold. Don't just stand there, move!'

The custody sergeant and PC Spencer gently manoeuvred the young man into the recovery position as Mark put in an urgent call for the doctor who arrived a few short minutes later. He was shown into the cell and quickly examined the prisoner. He glanced at Geraint and shook his head.

'I'm sorry, Sergeant, he's dead; has been for some hours. Anyone like to tell me what happened?'

'Nothing to tell, Doc,' Geraint said. 'I read the log when I came on shift and he was checked regularly during the night, appeared to be sleeping. When I brought breakfast this morning, I couldn't get a response, so I called you. What do you think killed him? Heart attack or something? Cos he seemed fine to me yesterday.'

'Not a clue until he can be properly examined, you know that, but there's nothing obvious – apart from the shortage of breath that is.' The doctor looked at the others in the room but no one laughed at his dark humour.

Mark Jefferies headed back upstairs, grateful to leave the distressing scene, and sought sanctuary in the incident room. It was nearly eight in the morning and he hadn't heard anything from Ben or Jack, but they needed to know about this. He picked up his desk phone and called Ben's mobile, hoped it was set on vibrate and he wasn't phoning at an awkward moment.

The phone rang a couple of times before it was answered.

'Yes,' DI James hissed.

'It's Mark, boss. We've got a problem. OK to talk?'

'Yeah, I guess.' Ben sighed. 'We're just about to wrap things up here.'

'Any luck?' Mark asked, not wanting to relay his bad news.

'Nothing unless you count a stiff neck, damp clothes and a sheep tick bite or two. No one's been near the place and nothing seen on the roads. So either Cavendish was winding us up or we were spotted, but it's not happening.' Ben yawned. 'What have you got to tell me?'

'Not good news, boss. We just discovered Cavendish in his cell – dead.'

'What?' Ben exploded. 'How's that happened? Did he kill himself? Talk to me, Constable.'

'No obvious signs of suicide, boss. Doc was here within minutes and seemed to think he'd been dead for a while. The custody officers checked him throughout the night, everything seemed fine, and the log records he was sleeping. Sgt Jones took in tea and toast first thing and couldn't wake him. That's all we know for now.'

* * *

When Ben and Jack returned from the stake-out with nothing to show for the hours of surveillance, a couple of uniforms took their place in the ruined sheepfold, but no one really expected anything to happen during daylight hours. Jeremy Cavendish's body had been removed to the local pathology labs but without yet knowing the cause of death, the internal investigation couldn't really begin. There hadn't been a similar incident for years at any of the local stations and this – the death of a key witness in a larger investigation – was particularly shocking. Any chance of potential leads had died with Jeremy.

'God, Jack, what a bloody mess.' Ben held his head in his hands and scrubbed his short hair. 'I don't know where we go from here, any ideas?' he asked hopefully.

'Not many, to be honest. I had a feeling it was all going too well.' Jack glanced at an open file on the desk. 'I've read through the custody reports and everything was done by the book. Cavendish was checked at regular intervals, was alive and kicking at supper time, ate the food he was given, then settled down and apparently went to sleep. No calls in the night, nothing. It was only when Geraint went in this morning that we knew we had a problem.'

'I guess we have to wait until the labs tell us what killed him. Maybe it was a heart attack, stroke or something, nothing to do with us, just incredibly unlucky.'

'We can but hope, it does happen. The duty doctor couldn't find anything immediately obvious.'

'God, what a mess,' Ben said again.

'Cheer up, boss, maybe the guys watching the house will be luckier. I can't believe this colonel bloke would abandon so many pills. He's going to want the money for them surely, they represent a fortune on the street. No way he'd just walk away, and as far as we know, he isn't even aware we'd arrested his boy, let alone that he's dead. I wonder why no one showed up this morning.'

'We don't know enough about any of this though, do we, Jack?' Ben sighed. 'We were just making inroads and now this. Perhaps the puppet master does know. Perhaps Jeremy had to keep in touch via the net. If he didn't make contact, maybe that rang alarm bells and the colonel's drawn stumps and vanished? We should have asked much more about the scheme – while we had the chance.'

Jack frowned and drank deeply from his mug, plainly thinking hard.

PC Bradshaw entered the room, carrying a stack of computer printouts on top of which was balanced a laptop.

'I think I may have something for you, Inspector. Do you have a minute so I can run you through what I've found?' he asked.

'Can't do much else, can we?' Ben growled. 'Come on then, let's see what you've got.'

Ben shoved piles of paperwork out of the way. Ian dumped the printouts on the table and fired up his computer. Jack snagged a nearby chair, pulled it closer to the desk, and peered at the screen.

'I think I've managed to find some correspondence records between Cavendish and the colonel before they moved their chats to the dark web. The conversations started about six months ago and it appears the colonel did approach Cavendish after the lad sent out numerous CVs in his hunt for work.'

'So, he was telling the truth?' Ben asked.

Ian nodded. 'I reckon. As he told us, they moved their chats to the dark web and most of the later stuff was heavily encrypted. Haven't been able to get in yet, but I'm working on it.'

'So, what have you got?' Jack asked. 'Doesn't sound like much to me.'

'I'm not convinced the colonel is the only other person involved,' Ian explained. 'I've come across mention of something referred to as, the "Consortium". By reading through the emails and chat room records I can access, it appears that a larger group is involved. There have been sporadic emails between the colonel and four others known as the councillor, the cashier, the conspirator and the chemist. I've been able to prove – digitally – that occasionally all five were in chat rooms together, but not what was discussed.' Ian tapped the keyboard and a mass of letters and numbers crawled across the screen. 'You can see the problem, though, can't you, boss?'

Ben stared at the meaningless computer scribble and chuckled. 'Not sure I can, to be honest with you, none of that means anything to me at all.'

'Somewhere in all that garbage is probably the key to the code they've been using and possibly, if we're really lucky, we might be able to pull out locations of the computers that the group used to communicate. That's going to take some work, though, I'm sure they'll have covered their tracks. They seem to know what they're doing; good at the cloak and dagger stuff.'

Jack flipped open a folder and read the notes Ian had made as he'd worked. On the first page was a list of names, monikers really, he read them slowly several times. Something was tickling his brain cells, he knew he could see something, but whatever it was remained elusive. He hauled himself upright and began collecting mugs, preparing to fetch a round of coffee. He'd almost made it to the door, when he slammed the mugs on top of a filing cabinet and marched back to the desk. He picked up the list of names again and began to smile.

'Think I've got it, boss,' he said. 'Look, these titles, they all start with the letter "C": colonel, councillor, cashier, chemist and conspirator. There's five of them. Five Cs, like the pills – 5c.'

'Of course!' Ian said. 'I should've spotted that. I'm trying to be too clever and missing the bleedin' obvious.'

Ben took the list from his sergeant's hand and read it for himself. 'Well done, Jack, you could be right. Cavendish fits the bill nicely as chemist, maybe the other nicknames aren't random. Maybe we are actually looking for a councillor, a colonel, a cashier and a conspirator.'

'Yeah, whatever that means.' Jack stood. 'I'm going for coffee, always think better with a mug in my hand. Good work, Ian, I don't know how you do all this stuff, but I'm amazed and delighted you can.'

'I agree,' Ben said. 'Excellent work. If you leave your notes, Ian, we'll go through them and perhaps in the meantime you can work on the code they've been using? We need to find out what these individuals have been talking about.'

Ian looked doubtful. 'I'll do my best, boss, but they've been very careful. Don't expect anything fast, will you? This is going to take hours, days probably and even then I might not crack it.'

'Just give it your best shot and holler if you find anything, anything at all that could be useful. Can anyone help you? Would an extra body be useful?'

'No thanks, boss, I'll find a quiet office and get on with it, I don't need distractions.'

Ian picked up the laptop, left the paperwork behind and made for the door, passing Jack who was returning with coffee. Ben called over Mark Jefferies and Julie Smith.

'Pull up some chairs, you two, there's a mountain of paperwork here that needs working on. If you can find your way through it without bothering PC Bradshaw, that would be good. I don't want him disturbed while his brain seems to be working in overdrive.'

'What are we looking for, boss?' Julie asked.

'Records of any contact between the five individuals on that list, dates, times, any patterns, you know the drill.'

They nodded and settled down to work. Ben and Jack reviewed the notes Ian had made and puzzled about the Consortium and the titles the members used. What bothered DI James was the unbidden thought that this shadowy group may have had something to do with the death of Cavendish, but how could that be? He was safely locked up in the cells when he died, none of these individuals could have possibly gained access to him. He tried to remember the riddle about something happening in a room which was locked from the inside and had no windows, but only succeeded in twisting his mind in knots.

Chapter ten

Stacey filled the kettle and put it on top of the Aga to boil.

Andrew Carr stretched his arms above his head and groaned. 'That was a great lunch, Stacey,' he said. 'Thank you for inviting me over. It's good to be able to see where you live. You have a really beautiful cottage and I love the garden.'

'Me too.' Stacey smiled. 'I was very lucky, my auntie Alice left Noddfa to me. I spent nearly all my summer holidays here when I was a kid, so the place has always been like a second home. Couldn't imagine living anywhere else now than on what I laughingly refer to as "my" mountain.' She placed a coffee pot on the table together with a couple of mugs and a plate of buttered Welsh cakes.

Andrew took one, bit into it and mumbled his appreciation. 'These are good, thanks, didn't think I had any room left after the carbonara.'

Stacey poured coffee. 'How are you settling in?' she asked.

'Pretty well, thanks. I'm renting a flat in Llanwrtyd Wells, not far down the road from you and it's comfortable enough. Great view of the river. I'd like a place like this, though, with a garden. I've always been into bird-watching and can't believe how many species you have visiting the feeders.' He sipped his coffee. 'Yes, I'd like a set up like this, very much.' He sipped his coffee.

'How about the job? How's that going? I've been reading your stuff, you're pretty good.'

'Thanks.' He grinned. 'I thought Mid Wales would be too quiet for me, but I'm keeping busy. Covered the last home match at Llandovery Rugby Club a week or so ago. They won in fine style and the after-match celebrations were mad, Welshmen everywhere drinking copious amounts of alcohol and all singing at the tops of their voices. I quite enjoyed the outing once I'd acclimatised and realised they don't eat Englishmen anymore.'

Stacey laughed. 'Wait until you go to a match they lose, they'll probably drink even more and sing even louder.'

Andrew helped himself to another griddle cake.

'Have you anything planned for the weekend?' Stacey asked. 'Saturday night in particular?'

'Are you asking me on a date?' Andrew spluttered, spraying cake crumbs and raisins.

'Don't be silly.' Stacey giggled. 'This is work. You know I'm investigating the rave and party scene?'

'Yeah, you told me.'

'Well, there's an upcoming event at a manor house halfway to Brecon. I'm thinking of going and wondered if you fancied tagging along? You'll be on expenses and I'm hoping it will be a good night. The illegal bash a few weeks ago was fun – even if it was against the law – and I wondered what differences there would be with a legal do. Bound to be a lot bigger than the one at Garth for a start, they're expecting a few thousand I believe. You up for it?'

'Hell, yes! I'd be delighted to go with you.' Andrew hesitated. 'I'm not going to get any grief from that copper of yours, am I? I've heard he can be a handful.'

'What rubbish! That copper of mine is a pussy cat, his sergeant is the one you have to watch out for. That's sorted then, good. If you get here about five on Saturday, we can arrive early and see how everything is set up. Should be a fun night, even if we are both working.'

* * *

A little after seven, Stacey heard her partner's car pull up in the lane and went out to meet him. Ben hauled himself out of the vehicle, locked the door and headed up the drive, delighted to see her waiting for him. He wrapped her in his arms and she leaned against him while he stroked her long, dark hair.

'Am I glad to see you, Pumpkin,' he mumbled. 'What a bloody awful day it's been.'

'Come in and tell me all about it. I've set the table in the back garden and there's a whisky on ice waiting for you.'

'You're an angel, you know that, don't you?' He reluctantly released her, wandered through the cottage and into the warm sunshine in the back garden.

The evening was perfectly still, not the hint of a breeze and the air above flowered borders was cloudy with dancing gnats. A few bees buzzed about, loud in the stillness, and a blackbird sang stridently from the top of a nearby tree. In the distance Ben could hear sheep and their lambs bleating on the mountain, and the occasional rattle of gunfire from the direction of the army ranges. He sat at the table, warmed by the yellow sunshine, and took a large gulp from the crystal glass, wincing as the spirit burned a fiery track to his stomach. Stacey emerged from the back door with two large plates of salad, a platter of cooked meat, a hand-raised pork pie, freshly baked rolls, and the remainder of the Purl Wen cheese she'd bought at Brecon market.

'I thought it was too warm for a heavy meal, so hope this will do,' she said.

'Perfect.' Ben smiled at her. 'I haven't got much of an appetite, to be honest, but I'm sure I'll be able to manage this. Looks like the best drover's supper I've ever seen.'

'So, not a good day then, Sherlock?'

'Dreadful.' Ben sipped his drink. 'We had a death in custody this morning. Sgt Jones discovered the body when he took in breakfast.'

'How awful!' Stacey said. 'What happened?'

'Not sure yet, appears the lad may have died in his sleep. He'd been checked throughout the night and the staff thought he was sleeping. We still don't know why he died. I'm hoping for a report in the morning.'

'What was his name?'

'Jeremy Cavendish, the guy we arrested on the morning of the raid.'

'God, Ben, that's terrible, he was only young. How on earth could this happen?'

'You know as much as I do and I have no idea. Might just be one of those things, people do die, young people too, so perhaps it was a natural causes thing. We can only hope so.'

'What else could it have been? Did he kill himself?'

Ben shook his head. 'He was found lying on the mattress in his cell, blanket over him, peaceful. I can see why staff thought he was asleep. The cell was last opened when they fed him supper and not again until Geraint took him a cuppa first thing and discovered him dead.'

Stacey thought for a moment. 'Could his death have anything to do with the people he was working for? Maybe they were pissed off at him for getting arrested, or because they'd lost so many pills.'

'Could be anything, but I'm not sure the "Consortium" even know he's been nicked. Anyway, how would they gain access to him banged up in Builth nick?'

'Did you say, the "Consortium"?'

'This is strictly off the record for now, Stace, OK?'

Stacey nodded. 'Of course. I never print anything you tell me, unless of course I can verify the information from another source. You know that.'

'Yeah, I know, sorry, but you can't blame me.'

'So tell me.'

'Ian Bradshaw has been able to recover some stuff from the net, which is where Cavendish met his contact, his puppet master. Ian discovered multiple references to a group of five individuals all using nicknames starting with a "C", and they all seem to be members of this Consortium thing.'

'The pills were stamped "5c", weren't they? That must refer to the group surely?'

'You'd think so, but it's very easy to jump to conclusions when you haven't got much hard evidence and if we're not careful, we'll become fixated on one idea and not uncover the real answer. I think it's too much of a coincidence though, not to be connected. Jack spotted it too.' Ben folded a piece of salted beef around a cube of blue cheese and pushed the parcel into his mouth.

'So who are they, these Consortium members?' Stacey asked.

Ben recited the monikers from memory and Stacey pondered while she chewed.

'I reckon the clues are in their names,' she finally said. 'Jeremy was the chemist, I'm sure of it, too much of a coincidence to be anything else. So, if we assume that's correct, we just need to find four people who fit the remaining names.'

'That's what I thought. I've been trying to work out if the names relate to what they bring to the group, rather than what they are themselves – if you see what I mean.'

'I do and you might be right. The chemist – assuming he was Jeremy – brought his knowledge, the ability to manufacture the drugs. Maybe the "cashier" bankrolled the project, or holds the money after the drugs have been sold, launders it perhaps.'

'He, or she, is bound to have something to do with the money side if our premise holds good.' Ben swallowed the last of his drink. 'Can't explain the others, though, I mean what is a conspirator?'

Stacey laughed. 'Someone who conspires – obviously. The planner behind the scheme?'

'Enough,' Ben protested. 'I'm tired. Let's talk about something else. I'll never sleep with all this rolling around in my brain, firing off random synapses. How did your day go?'

'Good, thanks. Andrew Carr, the new cub reporter, came over for lunch. Sam wanted me to find out how he was settling in, get to know him better. We've arranged an outing together on Saturday night. There's a large dance event halfway to Brecon and Sam has stumped up for tickets.'

'Your editor is buying tickets for both of you?' Ben raised his eyebrows. 'What's he up to then? Matchmaking?'

'Don't be daft, it's work. Information gathering for the feature I'm writing. This event is a licensed do and I'd like to have a better feel for the dance scene. Who knows, I might be able to find some more of your nasty pills.'

'Well, be careful, that's all I ask. Why didn't you ask me to go with you?'

'Cos you'll probably be on shift and Andrew's been to loads of these things… being younger.'

'Now you're saying I'm too old,' Ben grouched, eyes twinkling. He stacked the empty plates and carried them to the cottage. 'Come on, it's bedtime. You can't expect an old man like me to stay up half the night drinking, can you? You make the cocoa and I'll go up and put my bed socks on.'

Chapter eleven

The exclusive chat room on the dark web came alive as the remaining members of the Consortium logged on. The group had several matters to discuss, including the lack of a chemist and, as usual, the colonel chaired the meeting.

The cashier was concerned about the cash-flow situation. Little was coming in as the last batch of pills remained hidden by the back fence of the garden at the makeshift laboratory. The colonel had been about to make the collection when he'd received an urgent communication from the conspirator, warning him to stay away. All four wanted their say and the colonel had to repeatedly call them to order. They were using a dark web equivalent to Skype, no video, just digitally altered audio and they all wanted to talk at once.

'We need the money,' the cashier grumbled. 'We're maxed out with our suppliers and have customers waiting – important customers – the sort you don't let down. We must retrieve that shipment and fast or we're going to get severe grief and I for one can do without it.'

The councillor chipped in, 'I'd just like to say thank God for the conspirator. If he hadn't told us about the police surveillance we could all have been arrested.'

'Not a chance,' the colonel said. 'If that was the case, we'd already be in the cells. The police had our chemist in custody for a couple of days before he died and didn't find out much useful information, apart from the impending collection. Don't concern yourselves.' The colonel tried to calm the meeting. 'We'll hear if we need to worry. The encryption is bombproof, the police will never be able to trace us and the collection of the parcel is the least of our worries. What we really need to do is recruit a replacement chemist and find another suitable property for use as a lab. That's your department, councillor, so get on with it.'

'We've not only lost product, but the equipment too,' the cashier grumbled. 'Have you any idea how much that stuff costs? We've got to replace the lot, chemicals, the works, and the new lab has to be commissioned. We're going to lose months on this. The whole thing is a disaster.'

'A disaster would have been all of us getting nicked and that hasn't happened.' The conspirator pointed out. 'Let's tackle problems one at a time, instead of trying to fix everything at once. Colonel, can you arrange collection of the last batch? I think we ought to get it moved sharpish, tonight really. After a while the cops are going to give up on their surveillance and confiscate the pills. Surely you know someone who's capable of a covert in-and-out mission, after all, you're always bragging about your special forces training.' The conspirator sounded sarcastic.

'Of course I do! Recovery will be easy enough with the right man. I'll sort it out and by this time tomorrow we'll have our stock, then these important customers you lot worry about can be satisfied. That will solve our cash flow so we can construct another lab, but we still need a chemist to work it.'

The councillor agreed to help track down a replacement and still held details of two graduates who had been contacted, but not employed, during the early days of the scheme. A replacement should be no trouble and an empty building to use as a laboratory not much of an issue either.

The meeting ended positively. Each member of the group knew what was expected of them and would work tirelessly to complete their tasks. The stakes were high, there were fortunes to make and members of the Consortium were greedy.

* * *

The autopsy report on Jeremy Cavendish was delivered late morning without ceremony and Ben and Jack read the document together. They were quiet for several minutes as the information percolated inside their minds. The other members of the team glanced at the men, trying to read their thoughts, as anxious as their bosses to discover why the prisoner had died.

Ben sighed and handed the file to his sergeant. 'That's it then. No heart attack or stroke, nothing…' he struggled for the right word, '…tidy. Drug overdose with what looks to be the same stuff which poisoned Izzy Evans.'

'No, that can't be right,' Julie said. 'Surely he was searched before we banged him up?'

'Properly I hope,' Ben snapped. 'Jack, get Geraint Jones in here, will you? And Constable Spencer, he booked Cavendish in.'

Jack nodded and set off downstairs. Ben stared at the report in front of him, opened a drawer and pulled out a copy of the Izzy Evans' tox report. As he feared, the chemical analysis was identical. He leaned back in his chair and waited impatiently until his sergeant returned with the custody officers. They walked in looking concerned.

'Bad news, boys,' Ben said after they'd taken seats. 'Cavendish died from ingesting exactly the same MDMA as Izzy. Now, we arrested him early morning on the seventh, and found him dead on the morning of the ninth, over forty-eight hours later. Therefore, it is not possible he took this stuff before he was detained, so it follows he must have swallowed the drug while he was in custody. I want to know how either of you think that's remotely possible.' Ben glared at the men sitting opposite him.

Geraint spoke first. 'It's not possible, sir. He was searched when he came in and received no visitors, other than his solicitor and I can't see Mr Bowen acting as a mule to deliver illicit drugs to those in custody.'

'What do we know about Cavendish's brief?' Ben asked. 'I haven't come across him before; have either of you?'

Both men shook their heads.

'Cavendish must have had the stuff with him,' James Spencer said. 'He was searched alright, but maybe he had something… ah… tucked away. It does happen. And I'm with Geraint, I can't see a solicitor bringing drugs in either, certainly not to a police station.'

'We still need to check him out,' Ben said. 'See what you can uncover. Have a quiet word with Dick Nyle in Llandovery, maybe he's heard of him. Sgt Jones, I want you to speak with all staff who visited the custody suite during Cavendish's detention, ask why they were there, then check the logs again. We must be able to prove we took all reasonable steps to ensure his safety. What a bloody awful mess this is turning out to be. Have we tracked down his relatives yet?'

Geraint shook his head. 'I think he mentioned an auntie when he was in the cells, but he was an English lad, so I guess his family will be over there. We're still wading through paperwork recovered from the house, but none of it seems to be personal stuff. Ian has Cavendish's mobile phone, but hasn't been able to hack in yet. I don't know why he's taking so long, he's usually quick with stuff like that.'

'We have to up our game, gentlemen,' Ben said. 'This is just not good enough. A boy in our care managed to take class A drugs under our noses and die and we still don't really know who he is. That has to be our priority.' Ben got up from the desk. 'Right, on with it you lot and don't bother me until you have something useful to say. I'm off to have the riot act read to me by DCI Charlie Ambrose. You'd better hope he doesn't give me too much of a hard time cos if he does, I'm coming back down here to make your lives hell. Jack? With me.'

* * *

Light cloud cover made the collector's task much easier. The moon was almost full, but the murky sky blotted out most of the white light. He'd been surprised to hear from the colonel, until he realised the man was calling in favours. He hadn't said what was in the important package he wanted retrieved, only that recovery was vital. The collector had almost forgotten about the colonel, it had been years since they'd served together and he hadn't spoken to the man since he'd resigned his commission.

They'd met in the Shiite tribal areas of Iraq during the second Gulf War. The colonel was in charge of the desert base where the collector and his team had been stationed. They weren't exactly friendly, but enjoyed a good working relationship; indeed, the colonel had covered for the collector on a couple of occasions, saving him grief from the brass, even a possible court martial. Now it seemed he was expected to return the favour. Good job he was based at Sennybridge camp on the edge of the Epynt ranges – he wondered if his ex-comrade had known that. Maybe he hadn't and it was just lucky. The collector wouldn't have fancied travelling miles just to pick up a box, no matter how big a debt he owed.

He had been watching the settlement from a ridge overlooking the houses, tucked away inside a thick patch of gorse. The colonel had told him others were watching the package and utmost care would be required during retrieval, before adding that if the collector was caught, he was on his own – entirely.

For two hours now, he had watched, scanning the open countryside for signs of life. He'd already discovered a couple of Land Rovers parked some way up forestry tracks close by, and was certain he'd spotted movement in a crumbling sheepfold on the opposite hill. He wanted to be sure, though. He had no wish to get into any bother, no matter who he was working for, and lay perfectly still for another hour.

At three o'clock he was ready to move. Slowly he inched away from the bushes, body low, dressed in full camouflage gear, almost invisible in the weak light. At least he didn't have to carry any kit for this operation, apart from a pair of night-vision binoculars inside a large pocket, and a short knife tucked in an ankle scabbard – just in case. Within half an hour, he was probably no more than 150 yards away from the target. He took a breather behind a patch of bracken and peered cautiously through the leaves. He checked the sheepfold again and was sure he could make out the top of someone's head. The colonel had been right, others were watching.

Amateurs, he thought.

He reconnoitred the open ground between himself and the back fence of a tatty semi-detached house on the edge of the settlement. They were strange places, these little hamlets tucked away on the mountains. A lad in his squad referred to them as 'deliverance villages', a reference to the Burt Reynolds film made years ago. He smiled confidently to himself; couldn't see he'd have any problems with the locals, even if he was spotted. He briefly wondered what the package contained, why others were watching it and who they were – not that it made much difference. After a life in the army he was used to limited information, better that way – if you didn't know, you couldn't tell.

He spotted a shallow ditch not far to his left which seemed to run straight towards the target and he slowly crawled on his belly, using elbows and the tips of his toes to push his body forward. He moved so slowly it was like watching the hands of a clock, if you stared long enough you could see a minute tick by, but anyone on the opposite hill wouldn't be looking that intently, he was sure, so he paced himself and calculated he still had an hour before full light.

Eventually he reached the bramble-clad, wooden fence which separated an overgrown garden from the open farmland and he rested, checked the opposite hillside and saw nothing. Convinced he hadn't been spotted, he moved along in the shadow of the fence until he discovered a plastic storage box, about the size of a box of photocopy paper, tucked in the middle of a thick patch of brambles. Reaching out with his hand, he pulled the object towards his chest and discovered it was fairly light. The shiny plastic would be a problem reflecting any light, so the collector wrapped the box in a scrap of camouflage netting, before pushing it in front of his body as he made the slow crawl back up the mountain. As soon as he reached the patch of gorse bushes he knew he was in the clear. He made one final visual check of the derelict sheepfold, then slid over the crest of the hill and vanished. Mission accomplished – as always.

* * *

Ian Bradshaw was waiting when Ben clocked on at seven. He'd been working most of the night and was anxious to pass on information he'd discovered in the small hours.

Ben settled himself at his desk and Ian plonked himself on the chair opposite.

'Blimey, Ian, you look rough. Been out on the lash?' Ben asked.

'No chance, I've been here most of the night, trying to crack the code the Consortium have been using.'

'Any luck?'

'Not much. I've found a lot of chatter and a few meetings of the whole group but no idea what they're saying. Nicking Cavendish seems to have stirred them up. I'll have to cross-check on the web, but I reckon they're looking to recruit a new chemist. Seems logical to me they know we've arrested their guy.'

'Any idea how they will find someone else?' Ben asked.

'Probably the same way as before – online. I'll set up some monitoring systems and if they do make contact with someone, we'll know about it and might even get a name to work with…'

'You have something else to say?' Ben said.

'Well, I think they know quite a lot about our operation. I have a feeling the Consortium somehow knew about the stake-out and that's why you and DS Trent didn't see anyone collecting the goods. I reckon they knew you were there.'

'How can that be?' Ben asked. 'We didn't know ourselves until a couple of hours before we set it up. Maybe we were spotted on the way in, or I suppose they might have a contact in the village where the lab was.'

'No idea, boss, but I'm pretty sure they knew and can't see there's much point continuing surveillance, I don't reckon they'll be back.'

'OK. I'll let the lads know. Any further clues who these people are? Any IP addresses or anything?'

'Not yet, pretty much as I thought, their systems have been routed through servers all across Asia, then back via Eastern Europe.'

'It's possible to do that? Reroute the emails?'

'Yes, sir, it's not difficult. Anyway, I'm working on it but don't hold out much hope. They obviously haven't been stupid enough to use their own systems and the encryption programme they're using is top-notch. I haven't found much of a way inside at all yet, but I'm not giving up.'

'No, don't. Keep on, keeping on. Although, looking at you, you could do with some sleep. Go home, Ian, come back tomorrow when you've had a chance to get some decent rest. You'll be better for it, I'm sure. Find DS Trent on your way out, will you? Show him how to listen out for the alarms you've set on the system and then send him in.'

Ian nodded, hauled himself upright and slouched out of the office. He really did look as though he'd been up all night.

A while later, Jack appeared in the doorway.

'You wanted me, boss?'

'Yeah, Ian thinks our cover has been blown and the Consortium knew about our stake-out.'

'I know, he just told me.'

'Have you heard anything from the team up on the mountain?'

Jack shook his head. 'Nothing. Either they fell asleep and haven't woken up yet, or they saw nothing. Shall I call them in?'

'No, let's drive over. Find a car and I'll meet you outside in five minutes.'

* * *

Jack turned off the lane and onto one of the forestry tracks. A little way under the conifers rested an old green Land Rover. As Jack pulled up, two bored-looking police officers climbed out, stretching and rubbing their eyes.

'Morning,' Jack said. 'Good night?'

'Not really, since you ask, sir,' one of the constables said. 'Saw absolutely bugger all, nothing all night, quiet as the grave. Highlight of the stake-out was a badger wandering around at two, would you believe it walked into the front wheel?'

'Well, you can get off now. Round up the others and we'll meet you back in Builth for your report. We think we've been rumbled, so there's little point in hanging around any longer. Go and get some breakfast and we'll see you in an hour or so.'

Jack pulled back into the lane and drove towards the settlement, parking on the verge outside the empty house.

The narrow street was empty apart from a fat, contented looking, white and ginger cat, perched on a thick fence post, smiling at the men as they got out of the car. Jack ruffled the animal's fur as he walked past, then made for the front door, unlocked it using the new key and the officers walked into the damp hall. Everything was the same as they'd left it after the search teams had been in and Ben couldn't see the point of looking through everything again. Jack unbolted the newly repaired back door, walked into the garden and waded through long grass to the overgrown fence. He bent down expecting to see the plastic box of pills and couldn't believe his eyes when he discovered it missing.

'Boss!' he called. 'We've been had. The stuff's not here, it's gone! Must have been picked up during the night.'

'That's not possible, we had teams watching. No one could have collected the pills without being spotted. Not a chance.'

'Well, someone did, it's not here.'

Jack quickly checked the entire length of the fence and poked about amongst the thick briars before climbing over the wobbly structure to stand in the field. He glared at the ground as though he might find a clue, but the grass just looked like grass, no tracks or anything. Shielding his eyes, he scanned the mountain ridges surrounding the tiny settlement and saw nothing.

Ben joined him, his face dark with anger. 'Maybe those useless bastards did go to sleep?' he growled. 'There's no cover anywhere. I don't see how anyone could have got here without being seen. Bloody hell, Jack, Charlie Ambrose is going to have a seizure when I tell him we've lost a whole box of drugs. Why ever didn't we put something else out here and keep hold of the pills?'

'Because we didn't want anything to look suspicious and give the game away, that's why,' Jack answered, trying to calm his boss down.

'God, this is dreadful,' Ben moaned. 'All that shitty stuff on the streets and we had the chance to stop it. We haven't caught any of the architects of the scheme, or even know who we are looking for. The only suspect we did nick, managed to take some of his own disgusting pills and is now dead. I'll be lucky if I'm not demoted over this.'

'You won't be, you know you won't. The chief inspector isn't unreasonable and it's not your fault a couple of coppers couldn't stay awake long enough to be useful, is it? Come on, let's go and talk to them, find out what went on, then we'll go see Charlie together. I'm just as likely to be in the soft and pungent as you. After all' – he grinned – 'this was my project, don't forget.'

'Yeah, I know, but you're not the one cocking things up.' Ben sighed deeply. 'You drive and I'll think about what I'm going to say.'

Chapter twelve

DI James and his sergeant shifted uncomfortably in their seats as they faced the wrath of DCI Ambrose. Ben wasn't sure he'd ever seen the man so enraged.

'I thought a hell of a lot better of you than this, Inspector,' Ambrose raged. 'Whatever is the matter with you?' He glared at DS Trent. 'And you're no bloody better. For crying out loud, you seem to have no idea what you're doing – either of you. How could you let things get so far out of hand? I don't understand it, I really don't. You are both capable of great things, proved it over and over, but this? This is a grade one cock-up. You know the Super's on his way over, don't you? It'll be muggins here who has to deal with him, try to explain this debacle, although I haven't a clue how to even begin to do that, do you?' He frowned at his officers and they had the sense to keep their mouths shut. 'No, I thought not. Bloody useless beggars. So, apart from losing the only witness we had – when he took a drug overdose in one of our cells – and an enormous stash of ecstasy, what have you managed to achieve? Anything?'

Ben cleared his throat, he hated this sort of thing. He admired his Chief Inspector, had always tried to put in good work for the man, couldn't ever remember letting his boss down so badly, and was anxious to put things right – if he could.

'We seem to be making inroads into their computer systems at last,' he said. 'PC Bradshaw has been putting the hours in, pulled an all-nighter, he was dead on his feet. He's about the only member of the team who is equipped to deal with the digital side of this and I feel he's overdoing it, losing his effectiveness. We can't train anyone fast enough to help him with the workload and – if I'm honest – Ian would probably have to do the training.'

'What's he working on now?' Ambrose asked.

'He's trying to break the code the Consortium use in their chat rooms and is also working on Cavendish's mobile, but that seems to have been protected in the same way as the chat rooms. Ian says he hasn't seen anything like it before and hasn't discovered any useful information so far. At the same time, he's set up some sort of markers – I'm not sure of the correct terminology – on the websites these characters have been using. He'll know if they're communicating, but not what's being said. He told us there was a lot of chatter after we nicked Cavendish and seems convinced they knew about our stake-out.'

'So you see, sir,' Jack butted in, 'if they knew we were watching, they would have made other plans; would have been more careful.'

'Well, that's bloody obvious, isn't it, Sergeant? But how the hell they could sneak in past six coppers, six mind you, and not one of them see anything? Nothing?' Ambrose leaned back in his seat and folded his arms across his chest.

'Any news regarding the hunt for Cavendish's relatives?' he asked.

'We think so, sir,' Jack answered. 'DC Julie Smith had a bit of a brainwave. Although the services in the empty house were functioning, there wasn't a working landline and the mobile signal up there is crap. On the edge of a settlement is an old telephone box, still working, and she managed to obtain the call records. All the other properties in the area have their own landlines, so only a handful of calls are made each year. One local number had been called a few times over the last couple of months and we think it may belong to Jeremy's Auntie, the woman who arranged the solicitor for him when he was brought in.'

'Did he phone her when he was arrested?'

'Didn't make a single call from here, so we can't check the number that way. We were very surprised when his solicitor turned up.'

'Well, at least something's positive, the rest is a disaster. Tell DC Smith well done from me and tell the rest of them, yourselves included, to pull their damn socks up. Dismissed!'

The men didn't speak to each other until they were safely back downstairs and had a mug of coffee in front of them.

'Bloody hell, boss, that was a roasting,' Jack muttered. 'We deserve it mind, we're pathetic.'

'Charlie's helped focus our minds if nothing else,' Ben said. 'I don't think I've ever been carpeted like that before. What is the matter with us?'

'You know what I think?' Jack said. 'We reckoned the investigation was going to be easy. Discovered the dead girl, cause of death conclusive, found pills on her and a few weeks later I find some more. My snitch tells me where to look, we look, we find – in bloody great bucketfuls – we link other crimes, get a lead from Cavendish, saddle up to stake-out the house and catch the colonel. Job done! Only it wasn't. If you think about it, boss, nothing is ever that easy. How many cases have you worked on like that in the past, cos I can't remember one which clicked into place like this one did at the start?'

'Maybe you're right, but what do we do? Where do we go from here, because I'm out of ideas? If only Ian could come up with something a bit quicker. A hit in cyberspace would surely alleviate things a little and give the team something to work with. Maybe we need to go back to the beginning and start all over again.'

Jack drank more coffee then a slow smile began to twitch the corners of his mouth. 'OK, I have an idea. One problem at a time, right? We have plenty of staff available, but only one who can find us digital leads on the web and until he does, the others haven't really got anything to work on. What we need is to find another geek to help Ian, there must be one in a darkened room somewhere.'

'I don't know of anyone,' Ben said. 'There are a few who tinker, but none of them can actually do anything useful. I'm sure some of what Ian does is highly questionable, but I don't ask.'

'We need a tame hacker,' Jack said. 'I think they're referred to as "White-hats". Ian's a hacker, but works for us and not against us. I've often thought if he was ever investigated he might have a problem, but I guess he can cover his tracks too.'

'OK, so we need a hacker. Have you the faintest idea of how to find one?'

'Not a clue, boss, but I'll bet Ian does. Let's give him a ring. Then I'll chase up Julie, find out if she's been able to trace Cavendish's aunt. At least the next time we have to go to see Charlie, we might have something good to tell him.'

* * *

Andrew arrived at Stacey's house late afternoon, loaded down with camera kit and a large rucksack with what looked like a bedroll attached to it.

'How long are you planning to stay at the rave?' Stacey asked.

'Till the end, of course – tomorrow morning. Have to be prepared though, in case it rains. I like to be comfortable.'

'Surely the whole point of a rave is to spend the night dancing, not lounging around being comfortable. We're not going to a festival and you've got way too much camera gear. Don't forget, this is my story, you're only really here as a chaperone.'

'Aw, Stace, you think I'd nick your story? I'm hurt. I wouldn't do that, but one of my favourite things is taking photos of people and there'll be a large crowd tonight, plus all the stuff that goes on before, stage building, sound tests, even setting up the bogs can be interesting.' He looked pleadingly at her.

'OK then, but if you bring it, you carry it.' Stacey slung a medium sized backpack on her shoulder. 'Let's be off. I've managed to get hold of a vehicle pass – Sam pulled a few strings – so we'll be able to drive right onto the site and park at the back of the crew area.'

As soon as the bags were loaded, Stacey fired up her old banger and set off over the range road, turned left on the main A40 and headed towards Brecon. Andrew chatted on about other parties he'd been to, some licensed, others not and had some good tales to tell. Nearly an hour after leaving Llanagethin, Stacey turned into a wide gateway and drove along a narrow drive, twisting in and out of a mass of rhododendron bushes, thickly planted on each side of the track. Rounding a bend, the manor house appeared in front of them, glass in its many windows glinting gold as the sun lowered steadily in the sky.

'Wow!' Andrew said. 'I didn't know this place was here, you can't see the building from the road. Where are they holding the rave? Not inside, surely?'

'No, round the back in the grounds. The parking area will be there too.'

Stacey steered carefully past the end of the grand house, then gingerly through a narrow rear courtyard over rough cobble stones. Some of the small outbuildings were rented by artisans and outside one sat a small, elderly woman, working at a spinning wheel. She smiled and nodded as the car passed. Andrew began scrabbling around on the back seat, trying to drag his kit bag between the front seats and onto his lap.

'Sit still, can't you?' Stacey grumbled. 'Whatever are you doing? I'm trying to drive here.'

'Need my camera. I have got to get a shot of that spinner. I feel like I've tripped back in time.' He wriggled some more.

'Stop it, will you? Look, we'll be parked in a minute or so, you can walk back and take all the photos you want. Just be patient.'

The area behind the crew tent was already packed with vehicles of all shapes and sizes. A black articulated lorry was parked at the back and mini forklift trucks were ferrying equipment out of the container and disappearing with it to the other side of the field, while the heavily tattooed female driver operated the tailgate lift. An industrious crowd of people scurried about in all directions, carrying boxes, running cables and shouting into mobile phones. Stacey tucked her car between two four-wheel drive jeeps and climbed out.

She checked her watch. 'Nearly five now,' she said, 'so how about we split up and meet again just before kick-off at eight.'

Andrew checked the flyer and nodded. 'I'm good with that. Have you got your phone on you? The signal's not too bad here, so ring if you want me for anything. Where shall we meet?'

Stacey pointed at an embellished stone bridge sweeping over the river which bordered the estate. 'There, on the bridge. Have fun and good luck with your spinner woman.'

Chapter thirteen

Ben and Jack sat at a corner table in the King's Head pub in the centre of Llandovery, watching the evening crowd and waiting for the rest of the team. Julie and Mark arrived together and Ian brought up the rear. He still looked exhausted, eyes red, skin pale even under the subdued lighting. They ordered drinks then sat to catch up on various elements of the investigation.

Julie spoke first. 'We managed to track down Cavendish's aunt, lives alone in Llandrindod of all places. I've been in touch and made an appointment to visit her tomorrow. The number that was called from the old phone box was hers.'

'That was a good piece of lateral thinking, Jules,' Ben said. 'Did you get hold of his parents' details?'

'Yep. I've been chatting with Avon and Somerset Constabulary and they have informed the Cavendishes of their son's death. His aunt, Gwen Hammond, has also been informed. I've made an appointment to visit because I want to ask her about the solicitor she arranged. James Spencer is checking the guy out, but what I'd really like to know is how the aunt knew her nephew had been arrested. He didn't take advantage of his phone call when we nicked him, so I don't understand how Steve Bowen knew he was in custody, let alone turn up to represent him.' Julie took a long drink from her glass.

'That's my girl,' Jack said proudly. 'That's been nagging at me too.'

'I've been thinking about the new recruit,' Ian said. 'This is a touch left-field, but I'm pretty sure we'll know when the Consortium start talking to someone else online, so how about we intercept any new guy and substitute him with one of our own? If we could pull it off, not only would we have access to the encryption codes, but we'd probably find out who all these people are – including Mr Big – and nick the lot in one go.' He buried his face in a pint of bitter.

'You mean an undercover operation?' Ben asked.

'Why not? At least we can start online. I can pretend to be whoever they choose to fill the post of chemist and block the genuine replies. If we eventually need an actual person – well, we've got plenty of those.'

Ben thought for a moment before answering. 'In theory that's a good idea, but let's be honest, the only manpower we have available are coppers and I'm pretty sure none of them still play with their chemistry sets. The Consortium employed a kid out of university last time and we're all a touch too old, don't you think?'

'Not just too old,' Mark huffed, 'but too well known. In a small area like this, folk know most of us by sight. We'd be too obvious, surely.'

'You could be right,' Ben said, 'but just because the cookhouse was local, doesn't mean the members of the group are, they could be miles away.' Ben drained his glass. 'Another anyone?'

Jack nodded. 'I'll give you a hand, boss.'

He collected the empty glasses and followed Ben to the bar. When they returned to the table, another man had joined the group and was sitting next to Ian. He was in his late twenties, maybe early thirties and dressed casually in jeans and T-shirt. His skin was pasty, as though he'd never been in the sun, and he wore round, owlish glasses. He looked like a six-foot Harry Potter. Placing full glasses on the table Ben raised an eyebrow in the newcomer's direction.

'Who's your friend, Ian?' he asked.

'This is Todd. Todd Morgan. We went to school together, known him for ever and we share a house,' Ian said. 'When the sarge rang me this afternoon and said we needed some help with the computer work, I immediately thought of Todd. He's not working at the moment so has plenty of time available. He's good too.'

Jack glowered suspiciously at Todd.

'I asked Ian if he knew a hacker,' Jack said, 'so I'm guessing that's what you are Todd, a hacker.'

'Yep, that's me.' Todd grinned. 'Been a programmer since I left school, a software engineer basically, worked mainly for banks, until the round of redundancies after the financial crash. I was paid off and used the cash to set up my own business.'

'And what exactly is your business?' Jack asked.

Todd chuckled. 'I suppose you could call me an internet private eye. I find things for people.'

'What sort of things?' Ben asked.

'All sorts. Lost pensions, premium bonds, old savings accounts, people sometimes. If you know where and how to look on the net, you can track down just about anything.'

'And you know where to look?'

'Don't let many of my customers down,' Todd said, a proud smirk on his lips.

'Has Ian talked to you about this investigation?' Jack muttered.

'Nope. Nothing at all. Only that he needed some help with something at work and asked if I'd be up for it. Things are a bit slack at the moment, so I agreed to come along to meet you, find out if I can help.'

'I'm not sure we'd be able to pay you,' Ben said. 'I don't know whether my budget covers hiring hackers, so I'll have to run the scheme past DCI Ambrose. You'll almost certainly need to come in and meet him, and of course you'll have to be vetted before we can say yes or no.'

'No rush.' Todd opened a laptop bag and pulled out a couple of sheets of paper. 'I've printed out a CV you should find useful, relevant sections highlighted. I'll be around, so just holler if you want me to come on board. Contact details on the back.' He handed the documents to Ben, stood and glanced at Ian. 'You ready, boy? The car's outside.'

Ian nodded and drained the last of his pint. 'I'll be in first thing tomorrow, sir, so if there's anything you need me to look at urgently, send a text and I'll get on it.'

'Will do. Good to meet you, Todd, we'll be in touch.' Ben shook the man's hand and watched as the friends left the pub together.

The rest of the group finished their own drinks, then abandoned the pub in search of much needed rest.

* * *

Stacey and Andrew were taking some time out. The rave had really warmed up after midnight and nearly everyone who had bought tickets was dancing. The music was incredibly loud, the light display truly breathtaking. Thousands of different coloured lights shone out across the vibrating crowd and a cluster of searchlights arrowed bright beams into space. A large, glowing balloon, tethered by a thick rope, hung twenty feet above the mass of heads and illuminated happy faces.

Stacey took a long pull from her water bottle, then passed it to her companion.

'I'm worn out,' she said, wiping her lips on her sleeve. 'How on earth does everyone keep dancing like that?'

'Drugs!' Andrew replied. 'They take lots of drugs.'

'What, all of them? That's a lot of drugs, there must be three thousand here at least.'

'Not all of them,' Andrew chuckled, 'but a sizable proportion. The whole point of ecstasy is to keep you awake and buzzing, it makes you believe you love everyone. I'm sure that's one of the reasons there is rarely any trouble at an event like this. Ecstasy makes you feel good, happy and… well… loving.'

'As long as it doesn't kill you,' Stacey pointed out.

'Yeah,' Andrew admitted. 'There is that.'

A sharp, noisy clatter overhead caused Stacey to look up and she spotted a helicopter hovering over the site. It appeared to be preparing to land in a field next to the dancing area. At first she thought it was the air ambulance, maybe someone had been taken ill, but after it had settled on the grass she saw the livery was a silver-grey colour, not the bright red the air ambulances used.

'The next DJ making an entrance,' Andrew explained. 'DJ Daze. He's pretty well known and has probably already worked a set at another event. Some of the best guys used to work three or four sessions a night right across the country in the heady days of the late nineties. Not so much of it now, though, most raving goes on inside big clubs in the cities, not outdoors like this.'

Stacey watched as a tall, thin man jumped out of the helicopter, ducked under the whirling blades and dashed across open ground heading backstage, shadowed by a couple of minders.

'Things will get lively now everyone's warmed up and he's arrived. Drum and bass man, plays stonking tunes. You haven't seen anything yet, Stace. Come on, let's go and dance.'

'You go, Andrew, I'm happy to sit and watch for a while. I can't believe this is on until eight tomorrow morning.' She checked her watch. 'That's hours away! I thought I could dance, but this is ridiculous – with or without drugs. Maybe I'm just getting old. I'm having fantasies about my bed.'

Andrew laughed. 'We can call it a day if you like,' he said. 'Or you can go and leave me here. I'm sure I'll find someone to drive me home.'

'Are you planning to stay until the end?'

'I reckon. I'm having a ball and it's Sunday tomorrow, so I can catch up on any sleeping I need to do then.'

'Well, if you're completely sure. I'll stay for maybe another hour or so and if you're not at the car by three, I'll go on home. I've got enough stuff for the feature and between the two of us, probably some decent pictures too.' She laughed. 'We'd better have something to show for this evening out, or Sam will be moaning about the cost of the tickets.'

'Don't wait for me,' Andrew said. 'I'm definitely gonna stay until the end. I like to see the packing up and you can find all sorts of stuff on a dance floor like this in the morning.'

'Like what?'

'All sorts! People drop things while they're dancing, you wouldn't believe what I've picked up in the past, watches, jewellery, wallets, drugs, you name it – I've found it.'

Stacey smiled. 'OK then. We'll catch up tomorrow afternoon. I'll ring you then and you'd better answer. Sam won't be pleased if I mislay you.'

Andrew laughed. 'I don't know so much. He wasn't too pleased when I turned up looking for a job, he's still grumpy now.'

'He's grumpy about everything, it's not you. Go and have a good time.'

Chapter fourteen

Ben strode into the incident room and found Constable Spencer perched on the edge of his desk.

'Morning, sir,' he said. 'How's things?'

'Not bad, thanks. Better now I've gotten over yesterday's roasting. I've just come from DCI Ambrose and he seems to have calmed down a little. Any good news for me?'

'Possibly. Good and potentially dreadful in about equal measures, I reckon.'

'Let's have the good news first then, don't like the sound of "dreadful".'

'I've been checking up on Steve Bowen, the solicitor from Cardiff, and he seems kosher to me. I spoke with Dick Nyle in Llandovery and he says he's worked with him a couple of times. Bowen has apparently been a criminal solicitor forever and only ever handles defences, no prosecutions at all.'

'Not one?'

'Nope. He's the "go to" guy if you get into any bother, and can afford his hefty fees. Has a bloody good record too, gets nearly everyone off – even the guilty ones.'

'I've never understood how these people live with themselves, defending guilty clients. Did you manage to discover who called him in for Cavendish?'

'It was the aunt, Gwen Hammond. The Cardiff firm confirmed she called and also that they have handled her affairs for some time. What I haven't been able to find out is how she knew Jeremy was in trouble. Perhaps Julie and Mark will be able to answer that after they've spoken to her this morning. And that brings us nicely to the possibly dreadful part.' Spencer took a deep breath before continuing. 'I've been right through the custody records – again – and spoken with every officer who went down to the cells during the period Cavendish was banged up and everything checks out. No visitors, no problems in the night, didn't ring his buzzer for anything, so remained banged up until the morning when Geraint found him.'

'So how is that a problem? If he was checked on regularly, didn't ring for assistance and had no visitors, then the only problem we have is he wasn't searched thoroughly enough when he was booked in. Must have had some pills on him somewhere.'

'I agree with you, sir, but, and it's a big "but", there is an outside chance that we may have given them to him.'

'What?'

'The custody records state Jeremy was complaining of a headache before supper, so the doc authorised two painkillers to be taken with his meal. It is possible they weren't aspirin. What if someone swapped them out for a couple of the Es we recovered?'

Ben groaned and rubbed his face with his hands and glowered at his constable. 'That's a bit far-fetched, isn't it? Why would anyone here do something like that? I think you're making problems where they don't exist. It's bad enough we may have missed the pills when he was searched, but to suggest someone here gave them to him… How on earth have you managed to dream up that bit of fiction?'

Spencer looked hurt, this wasn't the response he was expecting, anger maybe, but not denial and he didn't expect to be made to feel stupid.

'You asked me to look through it all again and I have,' he huffed. 'I was the one who searched Cavendish and he had nothing on him when he was locked up, not anywhere conventional anyway and why would he smuggle in ecstasy? Most of our detainees are happy to sleep, makes time pass quicker. An E would keep you up all night, bouncing off the walls. The only people who had contact with the prisoner during the time he was in the cells were coppers. No one else. The log clearly records he was given two pills – which he took – and the next time anyone had contact with him was when the sarge took him tea in the morning. I'm convinced it is possible he was slipped something the evening before.'

* * *

Julie rang the bell of the narrow town house in Llandrindod, while Mark locked the car. The door was opened by a woman in her late fifties dressed in a dusky pink suit worn over a paler pink blouse; a string of pearls shone at her neck. She wore her tightly permed hair short and had a round, full face to match her round, full body. Standing barely five feet tall she looked up at the officers on her doorstep.

'You must be from the police,' she said. 'I'm Gwen Hammond, Jeremy's auntie. That poor boy,' she sniffed, beckoning her visitors inside. 'Would you like some tea?' she asked.

'That would be lovely, Mrs Hammond,' Julie answered. 'Thank you.'

'It's Miss, not Mrs, but please call me Gwen. Come to the kitchen and I'll put the kettle on.'

They followed the stout woman as she bustled along a narrow hall which opened out into a fair-sized kitchen with a large conservatory built across the end wall. Many orchids hung from the glass roof, planted in strange box-like pots, roots dangling towards the floor in long strands. Julie gazed at them in awe and couldn't spot two the same. Pinks, purples, magentas, yellows, oranges and at least twelve different shades of white. She wandered between the plants and examined the beautiful display.

Gwen noticed her. 'Do you like orchids?'

'I like all flowers, but I love orchids,' Julie said. 'I've never seen anything like this in Wales, it's like being in the jungle. Years ago, I visited an orchid farm in Thailand and they grew them the same way, in little wooden boxes, no soil or anything. Couldn't work out how they managed to stay alive.'

'Orchids are very strange plants,' Gwen said. 'Most of these are dendrobiums, the second largest genus in the world and more are being discovered all the time. They originate in East Asia and only really need to be kept warm and damp. I keep them fed by spraying the whole plant with diluted fertiliser. In the wild they grow on trees, like the moss does in Wales, symbiotic rather than parasitic.'

'You certainly know your stuff,' Julie said, 'but it must be more complicated than that or everyone would do it. You could sell tickets for a tour of your collection. It really is breathtaking.'

The dumpy woman smiled as she poured boiling water into a large, flowered teapot and set it on the table next to matching mugs. Mark privately thought it was all a bit over the top, but thanked Gwen when she passed him a steaming mug.

'We are very sorry for your loss,' he said. 'Were you and Jeremy close?'

'As close as most aunties and nephews are,' Gwen answered. 'I was very sad to learn of his death, he was a good lad. I'd spoken to him a few times over the last couple of months and he told me he was travelling around Wales hunting for a job. I thought at the time he'd have better luck in England, so many of our young people are out of work and no jobs for them.' She sipped her tea.

'He didn't tell you he was living close by?' Mark asked.

'I had no idea. I asked him once where he was when he rang and I'm sure he said he was close to Hereford, still travelling, chasing work.' She looked at Julie. 'It was you who rang the other day wasn't it?'

Julie nodded.

Gwen continued. 'You could have knocked me down with a feather when you told me Jeremy was living just a few miles away and had been there for months. He never came to see me.' She dabbed her eyes with a crumpled tissue. 'Oh, his poor parents, bad enough he died, without knowing what he was up to at the time. Do you think the business with the drugs had anything to do with his death?'

'It's too early to say,' Julie said. 'I'm sorry, I know that isn't very helpful, but when a death occurs in custody there has to be a proper investigation by the Independent Police Authority and all that takes time. We will keep his parents informed, though, and I'm sure they'll update you. When did you learn he had been arrested?'

'When he phoned and told me. I guess it must have been soon after you arrested him and took him to the station. He called, told me where he was, said he was in trouble and asked if I could arrange a solicitor. I called Mr Bowen and he went to see Jeremy as soon as he was able.'

'Can you remember what time he called?' Mark asked, glancing up from his notebook.

'No idea other than sometime in the morning. I was up and about, so it must have been after seven, that's when I get up, but can't be more precise than that. Is it important?'

Mark didn't answer, but asked, 'What did your nephew say when he called?'

'Only that he'd been arrested, was in Builth police station and could I arrange a solicitor.'

'He didn't tell you why we'd locked him up?'

'No. Not a word.'

'Weren't you curious? Surely you asked, I mean it could have been for anything?'

'No, I didn't have time to ask any questions and the connection was dreadful, kept dropping out. As soon as he'd asked for a solicitor and I promised to arrange one, he hung up.'

* * *

Mark started the car as Julie dropped into the passenger seat.

'God, what a place,' he grumbled. 'All those flowers, living hell for hay fever sufferers, and that awful china. Talk about overkill, bloody flowers everywhere.'

'Pretty amazing, though,' Julie said, 'growing all those exotic species in cold, wet Wales. She must have a hefty electricity bill to keep the orchids warm enough.'

'I'm not at all surprised she's a "miss",' Mark grumbled. 'I don't know of a single bloke anywhere who could put up with all that. Nightmare.'

Julie giggled. 'Proper bachelor, you. What is it with this phone call do you reckon? How did Cavendish get access to a phone after seven in the morning on the day we nicked him? The only way that could happen would be through us, but there's no record of it.'

'Maybe Spencer forgot to write it down. He's been running round DI James' ankles ever since he got here, far too eager to please. Bet you he cocked up and is trying to cover his tracks. I don't trust him.'

'You say that about all new coppers. You'll get used to him and he'll get used to us – eventually. Come on, back to the station. Maybe we can think about this another way, there has to be an answer somewhere.'

Chapter fifteen

Ben squirted barbeque fuel on smoking coals and created a small explosion, which made Jack laugh so hard he had to sit down. The others joined in, much to Ben's embarrassment, and he studied the label on the bottle in his hand.

'Says it's for barbeques,' he protested. 'Seems more like neat petrol to me.'

'I hope not.' Stacey giggled. 'The food will taste disgusting if it is. Come on, Jules, give me a hand in the kitchen will you, leave the boys to their pyrotechnics.'

Jack heaved himself off the wooden bench and wandered over to stand by his boss, still chuckling.

'What's your take on the phone call mystery?' he asked.

'Can't work it out,' Ben said. 'Maybe Spencer is trying to cover up a mistake he made somewhere along the line, but Julie says she's even checked the station's phone records and no call was made to Miss Hammond at any time while Cavendish was in custody. He didn't have his mobile, that was in property, and we didn't find another one on him, so like you, I can't get my head around it.' He poked the charcoal. 'I've asked Ian to check the mobile but he says he'll have to contact the service provider and that will take time. He still hasn't been able to unlock the device.'

'Could Jeremy's aunt be lying?'

'Why would she lie about something like that? And if she is lying, we still come back to how she knew we'd nicked her nephew.'

'Hmm, seems to me a lot of people know about a lot of things they shouldn't.' Jack handed Ben an open can of lager. 'The owners of the drugs must have known we were watching, or we'd have caught them red-handed when they went to pick up the pills, although how they managed to collect the consignment *while* we were watching, I can't fathom. If the Consortium knew about the surveillance, they are bound to have known we'd nicked their chemist. I hate to say it, boss, but I'm beginning to think we've got an informer. Someone has got to be tipping them off.'

'I can't see that. I mean, who do you think would do something like that? Me, Julie, Mark, the doctor? I'm not convinced.'

'None of this feels good to me,' Jack muttered. 'We should restrict information regarding the case, stop the chatter round the nick. Too many people know too much when they don't need to. Let's try to keep the important, sensitive stuff inside a smaller circle. If we do end up having to put an undercover officer in, that'll be dangerous, more so if this group get to hear about it. Just bear it in mind, will you? Have you run Ian's idea past Charlie?'

Ben nodded. 'We had a good chat today after Mark and Julie got back. He's approved Todd, so that should help, and he is happy to go along with intercepting, then impersonating, any future chemistry student the Consortium snag. We talked about maybe having to put someone in the field later on, but he says it's too soon to consider that option.'

'Next time you see him, ask him not to mention the undercover aspect to anyone. We can't run the risk of an informer, not when things start to get serious and I have a feeling they will.' Jack took a long drink from his beer can. 'Let's not mention it to Stacey either,' he said.

Ben was shocked. 'What are you trying to say, Jack?'

'Nothing at all, calm down. I'm suggesting we keep this quiet in all directions, just in case. Better safe than sorry. Anyway, Stacey doesn't need to know until everything's done and dusted, then she can write another front-page story.'

'What front-page story are we talking about?' Stacey asked, returning with a large tray laden with raw meat, Julie close behind carrying another covered in fresh bread and salad.

'You've got ears like an elephant.' Jack laughed. 'The front page you're going to write when us lowly coppers solve the bad drugs case with a flourish and we're all hailed as heroes.'

'Oh, that front page.' She pulled a face. 'Come on, boys, get cooking. I'm starving and we've done our bit.' Stacey poured herself and Julie a glass of wine each and looping arms with her friend, strolled down to the bottom of the garden to watch the swallows swooping after their supper as shadows lengthened across the mountainside.

* * *

Ian Bradshaw followed Ben to his desk when his boss arrived in the office at the start of his shift.

'Morning, sir.'

'You're eager, Constable. What can I help you with?' Ben removed his jacket and settled behind his desk.

'Well, sir, Todd's on board. I've given him Cavendish's mobile phone to see if he can hack into the logs while I've been watching the chatter on the net. I'm pretty certain the Consortium are talking to a new chemist. I've printed out the conversations for you and I'm monitoring the situation. I wonder how you'd like to play this now. If I could offer some advice…?'

'Carry on, I'll be interested to hear what you have to say.' Ben leaned back in his chair.

'I think what we need to do is "listen in". Watch the communications and learn as much as we can about the possible new recruit. If the group handles this the same way as they did last time, at some point the new recruit will send them a CV, especially if they sell the job as a research scientist in a small lab in Wales.'

'OK, so what then?'

'If we are crafty, we could hijack the real CV, snatch it out of cyberspace and send our own version. I could fix the details a bit, like date of birth for example, maybe advertise our man as a mature student or something, then seamlessly take over the messaging. Todd is sure he can write a misdirect programme on a system here that will allow us to talk to the Consortium, without them being aware of the substitution. We can't hang about making up our minds though. If we don't make the switch before they move everything to the dark web chat rooms, we won't have the encryption codes and we'll miss our chance.'

'OK, I get that.' Ben frowned thoughtfully. 'I agree. Carry on, gather the information and as soon as you think you've got enough to be convincing, let me know. I'll inform the others, but we're going to keep this a touch closer to our chests from now on. Make sure Todd knows not to go around shooting his mouth off and no unnecessary chatter in the station.'

Ian nodded. Ben noticed he very rarely questioned any order, just accepted what he was told and got on with the job. Ben wished he had a few more officers like that.

'Oh, and as soon as you get anything useful from the mobile, let me know, whether I'm on or off duty.'

'No problem, sir.'

'And find DS Trent for me will you, Ian?'

A few moments later Jack Trent appeared in the doorway.

'You wanted me, boss?'

Ben nodded. 'Take a seat a moment. Ian tells me the Consortium are in the process of recruiting a replacement chemist. He's watching the internet traffic and industriously learning as much as he can about the hopeful candidate. When he's confident, I've agreed he can try to take over the conversations. If he's successful, we may learn the code the group uses on the dark web.'

'That's progress. I'm impressed with Constable Bradshaw, very useful individual – if a little geeky-strange.'

'This is moving quicker than I thought it would, so I want you to work closely with Ian, learn about everything he does.'

'No problem.'

'If we do have to put an actual body in the field, I've been wondering about who to use. Mark had a valid point when he said most of us are known by sight, but you're relatively new and obviously not a local with that accent of yours, so…?'

'You thought you'd turn me into a student to infiltrate the gang?' Jack laughed. 'I'd be happy to give it a go, but I'm pretty sure I'm too old, we'd never get away with it.'

'I'm hoping we won't need to put you in the field, that we'll be able to snag the players on the net, but if we don't, I need someone clued up and ready to go.'

'Makes perfect sense.'

'I've also been considering what you said about an informant and – even if I detest the idea – what you said is a fair point. If you're shadowing Ian, you have the perfect excuse to hang around the station looking over shoulders and if you come across any dodgy behaviour, we can deal with it.'

'No problem. I'll get onto it. Anything else I can do?'

Ben shook his head. 'I don't think so, Jack, but we must be very careful from this point on. We don't know how big this supply network is, but it obviously has resources. If Jeremy's death was down to the Consortium, we will all have to be very careful.'

* * *

Stacey was taking some time out from behind the computer screen to enjoy her garden. She lolled on a free-standing, stripy hammock, a large straw hat shading her eyes. A bottle of chilled elderflower cordial leaked condensation on the top of a small table, a well-thumbed paperback in danger of soaking as the puddle slowly expanded.

The sun was hot, the sky utterly cloudless and the village quiet, the only sound a distant chainsaw, buzzing like an angry insect. Not far from her hammock hung one of the many bird feeders she kept in her garden and she watched as a nuthatch hammered at sunflower seeds held in by wire. Once he'd winkled one out, he zipped away to a nearby sallow tree, placed the morsel on a branch and hammered some more until the empty husk fell to the grass. Gazing across the mountain farmland her garden backed onto, she spotted a brown hare, lolloping slowly and easily over a rise, disappearing behind a thick patch of bracken. She sighed and stretched and remembered how lucky she was to live in such a wonderful place.

The sun crept higher and the temperature steadily increased. Stacey felt herself nodding off and tried to open her eyelids, without much success. A sharp clack from the direction of the side gate startled her. She struggled to sit up in the sagging canvas, finally managing to swing her legs over the side as Andrew Carr ambled round the end of her cottage.

He spotted her and smiled. 'There you are. Alright for some, lounging around in the sun while I'm running here, there and everywhere for that sadistic boss of ours.'

'Hi, Andrew. I wasn't expecting you, was I?' she asked.

'No, I wasn't expecting myself, but was close by and thought I'd pop in.'

'If you fetch a glass, you can help yourself to some elderflower – home-made.'

He headed for the kitchen and returned a few moments later to pour himself a drink. He took a careful sip.

'Wow, that's lovely.' He wiped his mouth on the back of his hand. 'Did you really make that?'

Stacey nodded. 'Any news, or is this purely social?'

'Bit of both.' Andrew dug in his pocket and dragged out a small plastic bag. He tossed it in Stacey's direction.

'Found those after the do on Saturday,' he said. 'Thought your boyfriend would be interested. They're stamped with the same marks as the ones that killed the girl. May even have come from the same batch.' He took another drink. 'I've also got some photos he might like to see, managed to snatch a few of shots of some dealers. A couple of shady looking guys were hanging around all night and not dancing much, so I kept half an eye on them. I thought I saw them dealing, found a hidey-hole and watched properly. Every time anyone approached, I fired off a couple of shots and now I've got a whole gallery of these guys and their customers, wondered if your bloke might recognise any of them.'

Stacey took the wad of prints and flipped through them, before examining the pills in the plastic bag.

'Why didn't you bring this lot over yesterday?'

Andrew chuckled and shrugged. 'Well, duh! I had been up all night on Saturday. Didn't get home until after lunch yesterday, hit the sack and crashed. I've only been awake a couple of hours. I brought them over as soon as I was up.'

'Oh, alright,' Stacey conceded and bent her head to study the pictures closely but couldn't recognise a single face. 'Can I have these?' she asked.

'Of course, that's why I came over. Sorry, Stacey, but it's a short visit, Sam's lined up a busy day for me, should have been somewhere else half an hour ago, so have to scoot. I'll catch up with you later in the week. Thanks for the drink, I'll see myself out.'

Stacey watched as he rounded the end of her cottage and heard his car start on the lane. She hauled herself out of the hammock, padded into the house in bare feet, shivering as skin made contact with the flagstone floor, and phoned Ben.

Chapter sixteen

After lunch, the team gathered in the incident room to discuss progress made and the recent leads.

Todd had finally managed to hack into the call records of Cavendish's mobile. What he discovered only generated more questions – awkward ones. It appeared the phone had been used to call Gwen Hammond on the morning her nephew was arrested, yet the custody records made no mention of the call, and no record of his property being accessed existed. On arrival at the station he had been searched and his personal belongings, including his mobile, had been removed. Jeremy had signed for their retention and they were locked away. On paper he had no access to his phone, but the records proved Gwen Hammond was telling the truth when she said her nephew had phoned her on the morning of his detention.

'The only way Cavendish could have got hold of his phone was if someone at the station gave it to him,' Ben said. 'Someone who had access to prisoner's property could have removed the phone and taken it to Cavendish without recording it in the log.'

'I'm sure it's Spencer,' Mark said. 'He has access and was the one who searched the kid before we banged him up. He was also on duty the night Cavendish died. I've already spoken about this with Julie and I for one don't trust him.'

'And I told you, you're like that with everyone,' Julie snapped. 'Sgt Jones has checked everything and there's absolutely no reason at all to think James Spencer had anything to do with it. You just don't like change, Mark, that's your problem. James seems OK to me.'

'I'm not convinced. I find this "lack of records" stuff highly suspicious,' Mark grumbled.

'If nothing happens, there's nothing to record, is there?' Julie sounded frustrated.

'But that's the bloody point, Jules, something did happen! Cavendish used his phone and… oh yes… he died.' Mark was on his feet, angry, glaring down at his colleague.

'Calm down. Mark, sit!' Ben ordered and waited for the hubbub to subside before he continued. 'We're not going to solve anything if we start bickering between ourselves. We've been making a complete hash of this investigation so far and I never want to go through another roasting from DCI Ambrose, so we must start making some positive progress. Two kids in our area have died so far because of these poisonous pills and we must prevent further deaths. We can only do that by catching the gang responsible for supplying them.' He glared at his team. 'DCs Smith and Jefferies, tell me how you got on with the photos Stacey sent. Anything to interest us?'

Mark sulked behind the desk, arms crossed over his chest, so Julie spoke for both of them.

'We have recognised one face.' She passed an enlarged copy of a photograph to her boss. 'I've ringed a guy to the left of that shot, he's in a dark hoody talking to a couple of suspected dealers. I reckon that's John Williams, Izzy's boyfriend, the last person we know who saw her before she died.'

Ben examined the grainy shot, squinting at the pixilated picture.

'I agree. Well spotted.' Ben peered intently at the print. 'I can't see he's actually doing anything, just standing close to those two shady looking types.'

'They appear in a few shots. I think the chap who took the photos was right, the pair look like dealers.' Julie smiled at her boss. 'Maybe that girlfriend of yours is rubbing off on young Mr Carr. He's only been here five minutes and is already sneaking around taking pictures of drug dealers.'

'The pills he found are the same as the ones we found at the cookhouse on the ranges,' Jack said. 'They're still with the labs, but they have the same markings. Should we go and see Williams again?' he asked.

'We could, but I don't know what we can use as an excuse,' Ben said. 'These photos only show he attended the rave, not that he was doing anything wrong. We can't keep knocking on his door or we might get accused of harassment.'

'I'll come up with a reason, boss,' Jack said. 'Leave it with me, I'll make a house call during the next couple of days. If I take some of these pictures with me, I can ask if he can put a name to the dealers.'

Ben nodded. 'OK, next item. Ian, what do you have to tell us?'

'More of a request really, sir. The Consortium's conversations on the open chat rooms are fast moving and although we've agreed to infiltrate the group, we urgently need a dummy CV for our man. I've made copies of the one Cavendish used when he was recruited, so we can lift the qualification details and tweak them a little, but we need to write the personal stuff – age, interests, etc.'

Ben cleared his throat. 'Right then, everyone, I need you to listen carefully. What we are about to discuss must remain confidential between ourselves. I do not want to hear any of this talked about in the nick or anywhere else. Do you understand?'

The team nodded in unison.

'I have already decided if the investigation dictates, and we have to put an actual body on the ground, it will be DS Trent. His accent clearly defines him as a non-local and being a relative newcomer, not as easily recognised. He has also had prior experience working undercover. My hope is we can wrap this up well before his input is required, but we need to invent a CV that will fit our sergeant, just in case. Ian, you work on that as a priority. You don't need to refer to me before you send it, but make sure you tell me when you have. I don't want to miss our opportunity to infiltrate by being too slow. Anything else?'

'Not really, sir,' Ian said, 'other than Todd has everything in place for the substitution and is convinced it's fail-safe. The Consortium will never notice the difference and Todd says he can arrange a seamless transition. With a bit of luck – if DS Trent's CV is found to be acceptable – we will be invited to move to the dark web and presumably be granted access to the encryption codes. Once we have those, we'll have access to everything.'

'Do you think we'll get away with it?' Ben asked.

'Can't see why not. The Consortium seem impatient to recruit a new man, so it might happen any day now.'

'Any of you have anything to add?' Ben looked at his team who shook their heads. 'On with it then, and remember, keep this confidential – it's important.'

* * *

The Consortium were online with the exception of the conspirator, but he often didn't join them. The news was good and the mood upbeat.

The councillor reported conversations with two likely candidates applying for the post of chemist. The online discussions were progressing well and very soon the colonel would step in and invite one of them to follow him to the dark web. An empty property had already been earmarked as a suitable lab and funds from the sale of the pills recovered from the ranges were being spent on equipment and chemicals.

The colonel was especially buoyant as the recovery of the last consignment had been so successful. He knew the rest of the group had been impressed and when the cashier sold the whole batch a day later, cash flooded in.

'How soon do you think you can have the new place up and running?' the colonel asked.

'Couple of weeks, three at the most,' the cashier answered. 'Everything has been bought and paid for and is *en route* to the lab. I've arranged for someone to be there to take delivery, someone who won't ask too many questions. I've also lined up a couple of lads to set up the kit so everything will be ready for our new chemist to begin work.'

'Everything on track then. Good. How long can we use the new place, councillor?'

'There are no plans for any development of the hall for the next ten to twelve months. A year or so ago, an application was made to convert the building into living accommodation, but was rejected by the local planning committee. It's been empty for nearly ten years now and I can't see anything changing. I've arranged for water and electricity to be reconnected and paid the contractors well, so we shouldn't have any problems.'

'Well done, councillor, let me know when I need to lead our new recruit over to the "dark side".' The colonel chuckled. 'The sooner the better and we can recommence production. I'm sure our customers will be placing repeat orders and we should have some stock available. Any problems, you know how to reach me.'

* * *

Stacey had just finished dressing when she heard her partner's key in the lock of the front door. She ran downstairs and met him in the hall. He looked tired and she worried he was working too hard.

'Are you OK, Sherlock?' she asked. 'We can cancel tonight if you like. It wouldn't be difficult to rustle up some supper, I've got plenty in.'

Ben pulled her into a hug and buried his nose in her coconut scented hair. 'You look and smell terrific and I want to show you off. No way are we cancelling. I've already changed and been looking forward to this for weeks. What man wouldn't want to wander around a posh garden party with a beautiful girl on his arm? Anyway, Charlie Ambrose will be pissed off if I don't make it. After the ticking off I received from him the other day, I'm surprised he's even talking to me, never mind putting me on the list for the Chief Super's annual bash. So glad I'm not expected to wear uniform.'

'Wish I could take a camera,' Stacey said. 'Bet there'll be some amazing shots to be had of the great and good of Powys. Who do you think will attend?'

'Top brass from the force obviously, a smattering of celebrities – and those who wish they were. I've only ever been once before, the conversation was deadly boring, but the food was good, lots of tasty nibbly things and copious amounts of champagne. Mind you, I didn't have you to escort me then, so it's bound to be better this time. Are you ready to go?'

'I'll just grab my bag.' Stacey headed for her office.

'You're not going to try to smuggle in a camera, are you?' Ben asked. 'Do I need to conduct a full body search before we leave?'

'You could,' she giggled, 'but then we're sure to be late.'

* * *

Ben and Stacey gawped at the enormous swooping lawn covered with many compact, marquee-like tents.

They were round in shape, all different colours and looked almost medieval with pennant flags fluttering from the top of each one.

'I keep expecting to see a knight in shining armour gallop out from behind those tents, start jousting or something. Isn't it pretty?' Stacey said.

'It is lovely, I'll admit,' Ben said. 'It poured with rain last time I attended and everything was covered in mud, but this is much better. Come on, let's circulate.'

The couple strolled arm in arm in the warm evening air. A waiter rushed over, noticed they didn't hold drinks and almost forced glasses of pink champagne on them, then moved away in search of other thirsty guests. A string quartet played under a colourful tented canopy and the music escaped from beneath the canvas to float between the crowd of well-dressed people. At the bottom of the lawn was a large, shallow lake, surface covered with water lilies, banks edged with yellow iris and meadowsweet. A few ducks paddled about in clear spots and a moorhen crept around on lily leaves, placing each wide foot gently and carefully, clucking loudly.

Ben sat on a wooden bench close to the water and his partner joined him.

'Do you feel better now, Sherlock?' Stacey asked. 'You looked so tired when you arrived at Noddfa.'

He draped a long arm around her shoulders. 'I am tired, haven't worked a case like this before, not when so much of it is happening online.' He sighed heavily. 'I don't understand cyberspace and have to rely on Ian to make sure I know what I need to. He's working all hours and not getting very far very fast. I'll be honest, all this makes me feel old, as though I'm out of sync with the world.'

'Not going well then?'

'Not terribly, but you know I can't tell you anything. You shouldn't know as much as you do.'

'But you know I'm trustworthy. Isn't it time you stopped worrying about confidentiality? In the years we've been going out, have I ever dropped you in it?'

'No, you never have, but you know me, I'm a worrier and us coppers are conditioned not to like the press. Can't imagine what I was thinking of, teaming up with you.' He leaned closer and kissed her softly on the cheek. 'At least I don't have to look out for pushers or pills at a do like this. I'm not sure string quartets and ecstasy mix, do they?'

Stacey laughed. 'That working class hero sergeant of yours would probably disagree. One of those little tents is probably stuffed full of high-grade cocaine, let's go and check it out.'

They strolled up the gentle incline towards the main gathering. Ben was immediately snaffled by DCI Ambrose, who dragged him away to chat with the Chief Superintendent, so Stacey ambled off in search of food. Digging in her bag for a tissue, she noticed her mobile phone nestling at the bottom. It was equipped with a fairly good camera and she'd seen other guests taking selfies. She smiled to herself, looked around, spotted Ben on the far side of the lawn, slipped the phone out of her bag and began taking pictures.

She wanted to be able to remember this evening, it was such an amazing spectacle. The vivid colours were striking against the emerald, manicured grass, and as the sun sank towards twilight, coloured fairy lights glittered on the canvas tents and branches of trees and shrubs. A pair of truly beautiful women wandered by, arm in arm, wearing gorgeous evening gowns, smiling, graceful, almost posing for a picture. The evening was warm and scented and large clusters of moths danced their blundering dances around hundreds of light bulbs. Stacey felt she could stay all night and decided she enjoyed posh garden parties more than raving. This was gentle and civilised and certainly less dependent on boundless energy.

* * *

Much later, Ben drove slowly through the midnight lanes towards Llanagethin, Stacey beside him, wrapped in a deep blue shawl. He wished he could talk over the police operation with her. He was certain she wasn't an informant and again felt angry with his sergeant for suggesting such a thing, but if everyone else had to keep quiet, it was only right he did the same. The annoying aspect was Stacey often had a different take on information, a different way of looking at things and had been very helpful in the past. He glanced over at her profile and smiled. He was sure she wouldn't betray his confidence.

'What?' she asked, noticing his gaze.

'I just wanted to…' he hesitated and changed his mind '…tell you I love you.'

She squeezed his thigh. 'And I love you too, Sherlock. I'm glad you have tomorrow off, you need a break and I'll need a lie-in, but you're always worth waking up for. You are OK, aren't you?'

'I'm fine, just tired. I've made such a bloody hash of this investigation so far, I'm surprised the Chief didn't shoot me on sight this evening.'

'Everything will work out, you know it will. You have a great team and nothing is ever solved overnight. From what you've told me, it sounds as though the Consortium is well run, careful and organised. They might have been at this for years for all you know, good at covering their tracks. You only found out about them after Izzy died. Anyway, enough about work. Your time off starts now.'

Ben pulled up in the drive of Noddfa behind his partner's tatty car and turned off the lights. Stacey kissed him soundly on the lips and he purred.

'Who needs posh fizz if they have you?' he murmured. 'You're better for me than any tonic I've ever been prescribed.'

'Softie.' Stacey climbed out of the car. 'Your bed socks are waiting for you on the pillow… I'll put the cocoa on.'

She laughed and ran up the front path before he could catch her.

Chapter seventeen

Ian and Jack sat together and read through the fictional CV, compiled using academic details lifted from one the genuine applicant had submitted. Todd had successfully blocked the document's onward travel and snatched it from cyberspace before it could reach the Consortium. The team had stuck with the name of the genuine candidate – Darren Redfern – but changed the date of birth and many of the interests. They all agreed that if it was necessary to put Jack in the field, he should be able to talk about himself. The original candidate stated he was a keen rock climber. Not only did Jack know nothing about the sport, but had a fear of heights, so his hobby was changed to DIY which also fitted well with the age increase. The team concocted a story that he was a mature student who had been anxious to retrain after losing his job in manufacturing. The address and contact details had also been amended. Satisfied they'd done all that was required, Ian sent the document with the tap of a couple of buttons and leaned back in his seat.

'That's done then, Sarge. Now all we have to do is wait for a reply.'

'Any idea how long that might be?' Jack asked.

'None at all. We don't know if the group check the site regularly and we also don't know whether we will fool them with this. I'm sure they'll carry out checks and if they smell a rat, we won't hear from them again. We know they've done this at least once before, and even though we nicked Cavendish, we didn't find a way to any of them. Hopefully, they'll feel fairly confident with their methods. How are you progressing with the stuff I gave you to read, your chemistry homework?' Ian grinned.

'I've been through the stuff a few times, feels a bit like learning lines for a play. I even understand some of it – but not most of it.'

'You may never need it, but if you do get sent in, you must be able to talk the talk in case you meet any of them in the flesh. Don't fret too much, I'm not sure any of the Consortium members will understand it either, after all, that's why they employ a chemist to do the work. I reckon the others are merely facilitators, organisers. If we play this right and manage to obtain the codes, we should be able to do everything from here.'

'Any luck with locations of their computers?'

'Not really, sir. Todd thought he'd got lucky with one, until he discovered the trail led to the local authority's offices in Llandrindod. He'd tracked it all the way from Asia, through Hungary, Estonia, then into the UK. He's sure it's a double blind, so he's concentrating on the others, but I don't hold out much hope. The internet is the perfect place for smoke and mirror tactics. There is still traffic in the chat room, but until we get our hands on the encryption codes, we have no idea what they are talking about. Very frustrating.'

'Well, keep me informed. I promised the boss I'd pay John Williams a visit this week, so I'll nip over there now, while we have a breathing space, but if we receive an answer, let me know immediately, and don't forget to inform the boss we've sent the CV. He'll want to keep DCI Ambrose updated.'

'Will do, sir.'

* * *

Jack took Julie with him for the interview with John Williams at the bail hostel in Llandrindod, together with a copy of the photograph Andrew had taken at the dance event on the twelfth. This time the front door to the hostel was shut and they leaned on buzzers until at last the door clicked open. Julie stood at the bottom of the staircase and stared upwards.

'I bet it's the top one,' she said, 'it always is. Still, no need to join a gym, the job keeps me fit.'

Jack chuckled and kissed her swiftly on the cheek. 'You look perfect to me, always have, so don't change a thing. Come on, I'll race you to the top.'

'Not fair, your legs are much longer than mine.' Julie pushed past him and set off up the staircase, Jack on her heels.

They arrived outside the scruffy door together and Jack hammered on the plywood. They listened, but heard nothing from the other side, so he banged again, harder, and was surprised when the door swung inwards. He glanced at his partner and pushed the door wide open.

'John?' he called. 'John Williams? Police!'

Jack stepped over the threshold, followed by his partner and cautiously entered the small flat. The place appeared unchanged since his last visit. He wandered into the untidy kitchen, while Julie headed for the bedroom.

'Jack. He's in here,' she called.

He moved swiftly along the tiny hall and squinted over her shoulder into the dim room. Williams was lying in bed.

'John, wake up,' he said. 'You've got guests.'

The lad didn't stir and Jack walked closer to the bed and shook the lad's shoulder, stopping abruptly when he realised John's eyes were wide open and sightless, already cloudy. He felt at the boy's throat for a pulse and discovered the skin was cold.

He groaned. 'Ah shit. He's dead.'

'Dead?'

'As a bloody dodo. Whistle up the crew, can you? I'll get hold of the boss. This is going to trash his day.'

'Do you think he's died from another overdose?' Julie asked.

'No idea, but it's possible. We need the doc here. Bloody hell, this was supposed to be a quick visit. I need to be close to the nick while all this undercover stuff is getting underway, not getting bogged down here.'

Within an hour John's body was ready for removal and an autopsy team waited at the local morgue. Ben arrived at the flat with DC Jefferies and Jack was released to return to the station. It was more important that he remained focused on his own section of the investigation than become embroiled with this. The doctor confirmed Williams had been dead for longer than twenty-four hours and found no obvious signs as to the cause of death.

* * *

Julie flopped on the saggy, comfortable sofa next to Jack and snuggled up. He lifted one of his long arms so she could wriggle closer, and hugged her to him.

'This is always the best part of any day, at home with you,' he said. 'I didn't know about "cwtching" before I came to Wales.'

'That's because the English hug, only the Welsh *cwtch*. Such a great word don't you think?'

Jack nodded and yawned. 'I'm not sure I'll ever be able to speak Welsh,' he mumbled sleepily. 'I mean, knowing the word for hug and being able to say good morning and good evening isn't going to get me very far, is it?'

Julie giggled. 'Depends on who you say it to. Could get you a very long way in some parts of Wales.' She tucked her feet up on the cushions and snuggled closer.

Jack stroked her arm gently and she felt herself relaxing.

‘The boss wasn’t very happy when he arrived at John’s place today,’ she said.

‘Are you surprised? He’s collected three bodies in as many weeks and not really any closer to catching this bloody Consortium lot. I hope they fall for the substitution. If we know what they’re talking about, we might be able to work out who they are.’ Jack sighed. ‘We don’t even know what sex they are, let alone anything else. Todd seems an OK bloke though, been working hard too, but he appears to be struggling. We desperately need that encryption code.’

‘Why didn’t we talk about this undercover thing before you volunteered?’ Julie asked quietly. ‘I mean, we’re supposed to be partners, but I didn’t know anything about it until after you’d agreed.’

‘Sorry, love, didn’t cross my mind. I’m still not used to having a partner yet, I’ve spent so long on my own and I’m not convinced I’ll have to physically go undercover. All that’s happening at the moment is we’re trying to fool the gang into thinking I’m their potential new recruit, and I’m not even doing that – Ian is.’

‘But you could end up going in and you’ve already said you will.’

Jack tilted her chin and looked into her pale green eyes, recognised the concern nestling there.

‘You’re worried about this operation, aren’t you?’

‘Yes, Jack, I am. I hated it when you were shot a while back. I’ve never felt such dread as I ran to the vicarage, so afraid you were going to die.’

‘That was only a flesh wound and I’ve got a fair bit of that to go around.’

‘That’s not the point, is it? It could have been much worse. This time you might be associating with really dangerous people, not just a mad, elderly vicar. You don’t know who this group are and the drugs scene is perilous. You of all people should know that.’

'And I do, my love. I ought to after working with the squad in London. I do know how to take care of myself and Ben won't let anything bad happen. If he's not convinced the scheme is safe, he won't go ahead.'

'I just wish you'd asked me, that's all. I'm not very happy with this and don't even understand why it has to be you, there are plenty of others who could handle some undercover work. All this talk of an informer makes me nervous. If there is one, you could be in serious danger if you're grassed up.'

'That's why we're making an effort to keep things quiet. Only a few people know about the operation and I can't see any of them as an insider, can you?'

Julie thought about it and reluctantly shook her head.

'There you are then. I'm a big boy, Jules, and more than able to take care of myself. There isn't a con out there who wants to see me angry, I can tell you. Now, how about an hour in the hot tub before bed to relax you. The water's perfect, I fired it up while you were cooking supper, and we don't use it anywhere near enough after all the effort I put into building the thing. And stop worrying. I promise I won't do anything without discussing it with you first.'

Chapter eighteen

The Mid Wales Times – 10th July
THIRD DEATH LINKED TO 'BAD' ECSTASY PILLS by Stacey Logan

A third person has died ingesting what police fear is a potentially fatal batch of ecstasy being peddled on the streets of South and Mid Wales. Police believe the death of John Williams, 22, from Llandrindod Wells, is linked with the death of two others in Powys, including his girlfriend, Izzy Evans. The pills have also been linked to incidents in Swansea and Cardiff.
In an ongoing operation, a large quantity of distinctive pills were recovered from a rural property being used as a manufacturing base. In an unusual move, police are offering a temporary amnesty to anyone in possession of these pills so they are able to hand them in without fear of prosecution. DI James said: 'These drugs are potentially so dangerous it is imperative we remove them from our streets. Anyone who has pills bearing the distinctive "5c" mark is warned they could be fatal and officers will not press charges

against anyone surrendering them at any police station.'
Deaths from similar designer drugs, as well as legal highs, have been climbing steadily over the last few years. Anyone with any information should contact their local police.

Stacey had been sitting in front of her computer screen for most of the morning and desperately needed a coffee break. The feature she was writing on the dance and drugs scene was going well, but local events meant it was a continual rewriting process.

She hauled herself to her feet, padded into the kitchen and put the kettle on. The back door stood open and sunshine streamed through the gap. While she waited for the water to boil, she leant against the door frame and gazed at the garden. The grass would have to be cut again soon and some of the flowering plants needed deadheading, but all in all her patch didn't look too untidy. She decided to drink her coffee in the garden. As she carried the cafetiere towards the door, she spotted her mobile on the table and realised she still hadn't had time to look at the pictures captured at the garden party. After she'd poured a cup of good strong brew, she switched on the phone and scrolled through the photos.

A smile twitched the corners of her mouth as she studied the miniature pictures. The garden party still looked like a medieval tournament to her, small round tents with their fluttering flags could have housed knights and their squires. There was a lovely shot of the two attractive women she had seen wandering the grounds, glasses of champagne in their hands, dressed in gorgeous, pale silk gowns, and another of musicians playing beneath one of the colourful canopies. The third shot covered a large area, but the screen was too small to appreciate it properly, so she collected her laptop from the office and waited while the sequence uploaded.

Working her way through the photographs, she was surprised she'd taken so many. There was one of Ben's back as he stood chatting with the Chief Superintendent, DCI Charlie Ambrose by his side, and more of the entire area taken just before twilight. In the middle of one of the landscape shots was a face she recognised, Robert Evans, Izzy's father. She couldn't remember seeing him there and wondered how he'd got an invite. The other guests all seemed to be local bigwigs, community leaders, chairman of the council, health professionals, a few lesser known celebrities and local sports stars. Robert was standing next to a short woman who was not his wife and Stacey didn't recognise her. Seeing him reminded her it had been a while since the Izzy Evans Trust had been launched and she wondered how it was going. Finishing her coffee, she returned to her office carrying the laptop with her.

She flipped through the box of business cards on her desk, found the one belonging to Robert Evans and called his office number. After explaining to the secretary who she was, she was eventually put through.

'Ms Logan. How are you?' Robert asked.

'Fine thanks, Mr Evans. How are you and your wife managing?'

'Not too badly. It's been very difficult to get through this awful patch, but setting up the trust has helped Mair enormously, given her something else to concentrate on. The piece you wrote in the paper generated a tremendous response. I meant to call to say thank you, but I've been very busy since I returned to the UK, what with one thing and another.' His voice tailed off.

'Is the trust going well?'

'Better than I thought it would. Several local companies have been in touch to offer their support, as well as a couple of drug agencies and the council. We've even been offered grants and one or two people have made remarkably generous donations. Mair is working on setting up a self-help group, somewhere parents and young people can go to discuss their drug abuse problems.' He hesitated. 'I read about John Williams' death in the paper. Was he really killed by the same drugs? You seemed to link the deaths in your article.'

'The police are convinced ecstasy was responsible, hence the amnesty. You might like to consider asking an officer to attend one of your meetings, I'm sure they'd be happy to provide someone.'

'That's not a bad idea, I'll pass it on to my wife.'

'Did I see you at the garden party last Sunday evening? I was there with DI James.'

'Yes, I was. I thought I saw you, but the light was going by then and I got caught up. DCI Ambrose invited me, thought I could make a few useful contacts for the trust. Very good of him to think of us. Unfortunately, Mair didn't feel up to it, but the Chief Inspector wasn't wrong. I bumped into Llandovery Rugby Team's captain and he was very keen to help, said he'd get us a mention in the next match programme.'

'I'm really glad everything is going so well,' Stacey said. 'Don't forget, if you arrange any events let me know and I'll do what I can to publicise them for you.'

* * *

Todd and Julie worked side by side in one corner of the conference room. They'd spent most of the day reading through a mountain of paperwork spilled out by the computers. Julie was a fast learner and Todd had been able to teach her what to look for, but without the code, the actual conversations between members of the Consortium still eluded them. They concentrated on early contacts between Cavendish and an individual referred to as the councillor. The colonel didn't seem to have been part of the early discussions and only joined in shortly before conversations moved to the dark web.

'This would be much more productive if we could work on the recent stuff,' Julie grumbled. 'I can't see much point in going over this lot. Jeremy thought he was applying for a proper job and his emails reflect that. This councillor person doesn't mention anything about the true nature of the recruitment either. Not until the colonel gets involved does everything move to the dark web and we can't access any of that.'

'Frustrating, isn't it?' Todd chuckled. 'I spend hours working with material similar to this, like a crazy word puzzle you can't solve, but we can glean a lot of information from the early discussions. For example, I'm pretty sure the councillor is female.'

'Really?' Julie was surprised. 'How did you arrive at that conclusion?'

'Mainly by the words the individual used. Look at this section where it says, "It would be lovely if you agreed to join the company." That doesn't sound like a phrase a man would use. There's another example somewhere.' He flipped through the pile of printouts. 'Here we are, "The directors are delighted to have found a young man with your qualifications." Would a man refer to another man as young or say he was delighted? I'm not sure he would in business correspondence, and there are lots of other examples. I'm certain the councillor is female.'

Julie examined the sections in the printout Todd had highlighted and read them through carefully.

'I think you're right, doesn't sound like a man. That's impressive, Todd. I'm not sure how it helps us, but anything the least bit positive will cheer the boss up.'

They fell silent as they immersed themselves in the pile of electronic communication. Todd got to his feet, stretched and went in search of fresh coffee. When he returned he found Julie staring out of the large picture window. She looked as though her mind was completely elsewhere and didn't acknowledge his return.

'You OK?' Todd asked.

She turned away from the window and returned to the paper strewn desk.

'I'm fine. Confused, that's all… and worried, if I'm honest.'

'What about?'

'The undercover thing. I'm afraid it will be dangerous.'

'Not yet it won't and maybe never. As soon as we get hold of the encryption code we can read all the rest of the stuff and, with a bit of luck, work out who these people are, then it won't be necessary for anyone to go into the lion's den.'

'Terms like "lion's den" don't make me feel any better at all. Honestly, Todd, we still haven't worked out what happened with this phone call thing. You proved Cavendish's phone was used to call his aunt after we locked him up. The aunt confirmed she did receive a call and the records back that up, but we have no idea how that was possible. Only police officers had access to Jeremy's stuff, yet the records show nothing left the property store.'

'You have a problem there, I'll admit, but it could be as simple as poor record keeping and no one wants to own up to it. There was only a single call made and the result was that a solicitor arrived at the station to represent Cavendish. No actual harm was caused by it.'

'Feels wrong though. Mistakes like that shouldn't happen and it proves we have faults in our system. We can't ask Jeremy because he's dead and we can't figure out how that happened either.' She sighed miserably. 'Now John Williams is dead. I can't help thinking the Consortium is larger and much better organised than we think. What if they were responsible for those deaths?'

'They can't be,' Todd said. 'How could anyone have got to Jeremy to kill him? You had him locked up.'

'Like we had his property locked up and someone managed to get to that, didn't they?'

The door of the room flew open and Ian dashed in. 'Todd, I need you. The colonel's been in touch and we're about to move to the dark web chat room. An extra set of eyes will be useful. Julie, can you round up DS Trent and get him to come downstairs? I'm working in a room at the end of the custody suite, no distractions down there.'

Chapter nineteen

The small team clustered round the desk, straining to see the screen. Todd quickly set up another laptop and duplicated the information so they could spread out and work more comfortably. An email was displayed.

To: darrenredfern@hotmail.com
From: thecolonel@yahoo.com
Subject: Job vacancy

I have been passed your details by one of my colleagues together with your CV. The board is very impressed with your qualifications and feel you would be well suited for the available position.
As you are aware, we have a vacancy as a research assistant in a small, privately run laboratory in Mid Wales, working within the pharmaceutical industry. The company's aim is to develop medicines to help clinically obese patients lose weight. We are considered to be leaders in the field.
Our work is sensitive and we have many competitors who would like access to our research. Therefore, I invite you to follow me online to a secure chat room

before I provide any further details. Future correspondence will be encrypted for security reasons. If you are interested in accepting the position, please download the attachment and agree to the terms and conditions regarding confidentiality.

'So far so good,' Jack said. 'Someone go and find DI James, he should be here. Looks as though the Consortium have fallen for it, now we should be able to get things moving.'

Todd and Ian concentrated on the screens and – as far as Jack was concerned – spoke in tongues as they discussed the download. From what he could make out, the pair seemed to be arguing over what their next step should be.

He interrupted them. 'Come on, boys, surely all we have to do now is download the attachment, or whatever, and we'll have the code.'

'In theory yes, sir,' Ian said, 'but we want to be absolutely certain the Consortium can't trace our equipment and isn't sending us a virus. Todd has set up the system to be secure, but we need to be certain it's fail-safe.'

'What's the worst that can happen?' Jack asked.

'They'd know we're onto them,' Todd said, 'and of course a virus would destroy our kit. If we cock this up, we may never get another chance. Even if we obtain the code, that's not the end of it. I'm convinced if they smell anything off, they'll vanish, we'll be right back where we started and all this work will have been a monumental waste of time.'

The computer experts resumed their lively discussion while Jack reread the email from the Colonel. A few moments later, Ben entered the room and the group made space for him at the desk.

He stared at the screen, the hint of a smile on his face. 'What do you advise, Ian?'

'I guess all we can do is give it a go,' Ian said, 'but you need to be aware that if this goes wrong, we'll lose everything and the Consortium will be tipped off. I'm a hundred per cent sure they won't be able to trace who we are, but they could smell a rat and pull the plug.'

'We haven't got any other option, so do it,' Ben ordered.

Ian shot his cuffs like a pianist before playing a piece of music, pulled himself closer to the keyboard and tapped a couple of keys before leaning back in his chair.

All eyes focused on the glowing screen. Minutes dragged as nothing happened. The team held their collective breath and waited. Half an hour later, they were still waiting, worried they had been caught out and gradually the pent-up anticipation changed to a feeling of anticlimax. Ben glanced at his watch. It was eight o'clock and he should have been at Stacey's ten minutes ago. He pulled his mobile out of his pocket and sent her a quick text telling her he'd been delayed and may not be able to make it over at all. As he pushed the send button, a cheer went up behind him.

'They've bought it! Fantastic!' Todd leapt to his feet and pounded Ian heartily on the back. 'Well done, boy, we've done it. Look at that beautiful code, what a piece of work. Now we can decode the communications we've amassed.'

Ben dashed to the desk and peered over his constable's shoulder as Ian stared at the screen, a wide grin plastered on his face.

'What's next?' Ben asked.

'I guess we have to accept the job… or not,' Ian said. 'Let's get a reply out as fast as we can. We have to look keen, our mature student is out of work and would be anxious to find out more, like what the wages are, where the job is. We can ask questions, just have to make them look convincing.'

Ten minutes later, the team had composed a reply and watched as Ian typed it ready for sending.

To: thecolonel@yahoo.com
From: darrenredfern@hotmail.com
Subject: Job Vacancy

Thank you for your email. I confirm I have read the terms and conditions you provided and am happy to accept them. I am very pleased to have been offered the position of Research Assistant and am available to commence work almost immediately.
I would be grateful if you could confirm the salary I can expect to receive, location of the lab and start date. I confirm I am able to relocate from England, but will require some time to find suitable accommodation and arrange to move. I assume you will require a face-to-face meeting before I take up the post.
Once again, I thank you for the opportunity you have offered me and look forward to hearing from you soon.

Ben and Jack read the email through several times, Julie peering over their shoulders.

'Send it, Ian,' Ben said, and watched as the communication disappeared into cyberspace. Then, more waiting.

The screen stayed stubbornly blank. They were expecting an instant reply, but after an hour nothing had come through.

'They're probably checking things out,' Todd said. He tapped away on his own laptop and was able to log into the chat room on the dark web.

'Look, guys, the chat room's full, they're having a meeting. Now we have the code we ought to be able to read what they're saying.' He tapped some more and the meaningless scribble covering the screen dissolved and was replaced with readable text. 'Seems like they're having a bit of a set-to. The conspirator doesn't appear very happy. Here look.' Todd pointed to the text. 'He's asking for a cooling off period, doesn't want them rushing into anything. There… they've agreed to wait until they have had time to discuss whatever is bothering them properly. We've picked up halfway through a conversation and… bummer, they've logged off.'

'So where does that leave us?' Jack asked.

'Ian and I can monitor the chat room overnight, but I'd be surprised if we receive anything else before tomorrow. You lot might as well go home and get some rest.'

'Shouldn't Jack stay?' Ben asked.

'No reason why he should, sir,' Ian answered. 'We have your contact numbers and if anything changes we'll get in touch, neither of you are far away. The Consortium won't expect their new recruit to be glued to his computer, so it shouldn't matter if we don't reply instantly.'

Ben eventually agreed and reasoned it was important his team should have some quality rest. Todd and Ian assured him they were capable of monitoring the chat room during the night and promised to spend the time usefully, decoding the masses of previous contacts they'd collected since the start of the investigation, ready for the team to work through in the morning.

The meeting broke up, leaving the geeks in the dimly lit, quiet room behind the cells while the rest made their way home; Jack and Julie to their cottage under the Epynt Mountain and Ben to his bachelor pad in the town. It was too late now to go to Stacey's and he didn't want to disturb her. As he drove away from the station, he felt positive for the first time in weeks, convinced they had a good chance of infiltrating the Consortium and discovering who the members were.

Chapter twenty

The conspirator sat in his car and stared across the open mountain land of the MoD firing ranges. He hadn't been sleeping well lately and had taken to driving up to the mountain in the early morning and late evening. He preferred sunsets to sunrises. Sunrise meant he had to face another day of pretence; sunset meant he had managed to survive another day.

Soft, salmon pinks with tinges of crimson and pale yellow began to streak the sky, then the sun rose, illuminating the gap between the land and heavy gathering clouds. A gentle breeze became a stiff wind and blew in trains of clouds which rapidly duplicated like a virus in a Petri dish. Far across the open expanse, the first hesitant flash of lightning traced the edges of thick clouds, and through the open window the conspirator heard a distant grumble of thunder.

The sky matched his mood, he felt as though a personal storm was coming and didn't know how to stop it. The wind picked up and drove the storm towards him, then the rain began, smothering the new day before it really had time to get going. Huge raindrops pounded the car's roof and windscreen, obliterating the view, water pouring in through the cracked window. The conspirator wound it closed and concentrated on the sound of the rain, a mad, deafening percussion which went on and on. He flicked on the windscreen wipers, but each time the improved visibility was fleeting. He wished he could wipe away some of the shit he'd got himself into so easily.

The scheme had seemed easy enough in the beginning, hand over a little information for a lot of money and who couldn't do with more money? Trouble was, things had escalated and now he couldn't control the situation. The other members of the Consortium were powerful, wealthy people who were much cleverer than he was. He'd tried to withdraw, but the colonel wouldn't let him, threatened to ruin him if he didn't continue to play ball. Remembering his guilty secret, his one, stupid indiscretion, made him shiver violently. If any of it ever came out, he would be ruined. He'd rather be dead. He wished he'd never met the colonel, or any of the others; that he'd never gotten involved – not that he'd really had much of a choice. He had no idea what to do now. He was still in much the same position, the alternative too dreadful to think about.

The rain eased and he climbed out of the car, watching as the storm chased away towards the middle of the ranges and behind it the sun tried again. Even this early he could feel warmth in the yellow light and it fortified him. It wouldn't go on forever, he reasoned, he'd been planning his escape for a while now, just needed to amass a little more money.

* * *

A smaller team congregated in the dark room behind the cells. Ben had sent James Spencer and Mark Jefferies upstairs to handle work generated by the recent death of John Williams. He hoped if they spent more time together, they would get to know each other and improve the mood in the station. For some reason Mark had really taken a dislike to the newcomer and his hostility was beginning to cause problems. It also seemed sensible to restrict knowledge of the undercover operation, even inside the team. Jack had every right to be cautious if he was about to undertake such a dangerous mission, it was potentially his neck at risk.

The room was hot and stuffy. Along one wall was a garden lounger complete with a couple of tatty looking cushions and a grey, standard issue blanket.

'Tell me you haven't been sleeping in here!' Ben exclaimed, stepping over the threshold.

'Well, yes, sir,' Ian admitted. 'We needed to monitor things throughout the night, so Todd and I worked shifts, one slept, the other watched.'

'I admire your dedication, but we'll have to sort something else out, you can't keep sleeping in here, it's ridiculous.' Ben folded the lounger, leant it against the wall and sat next to Ian who was peering at the computer screen.

'Do you have anything to show for your hard work?' Ben asked.

'Not much, a single communication from the colonel informing the new recruit there was no need to meet in person as he was in North Africa.'

'Is that where the colonel really is?'

Ian shrugged. 'No idea, but he said the post will be ready for Darren to take up in about four weeks and wanted to confirm that the start date of Monday 18th August would be acceptable. Nothing dodgy has been mentioned at all and no other consortium members have been online since yesterday. We haven't sent a reply yet.'

'OK. Work with Jack, compose an email and send it, then go home, have a shower, eat some breakfast and get at least three hours sleep in a proper bed before you even consider coming back in. Understood?'

'Yes, sir.'

'Todd, how about the past communications, now we have the code. How is that going?'

'Unfortunately, not as well as you'd like. There are lots of meetings, but very little of their communication is via the keyboard. I can tell who's online, when and for how long, but can't capture any content. It's starting to look as though they have some form of Skype and are speaking to each other, rather than typing.'

'Can we get into that at all?' Ben asked. 'If we can't work out what has been said, maybe we can hear what they talk about in the future.'

'No luck so far.' Todd rubbed his eyes. 'I'm pretty sure they've only supplied us with part of the code. We can email them and vice versa and we can decode anything sent using that method. This Skype-like device uses a different encryption again. I'd love to know who engineered their system, I've never seen anything quite like this before and as Ian said – I'm bloody good!'

Ben chuckled. 'And obviously very modest too, aren't you, boy? So, what do you advise?'

'Carry on the way we're going – monitor the site closely. I've set up an alarm on the system which will automatically call our mobiles if something comes in, that way we can get some sleep. Even hackers like to see daylight every now and again and this room's starting to close in on me.'

'What about the computers in here, do they need to be left on?'

'Be a good idea. The system's password protected so no one can gain access to anything.' He glanced across at Ian who was composing Jack's reply. 'Want a lift?'

Ian grinned and nodded, finished the email, grabbed his jacket and set off after Todd.

Jack raised an eyebrow in Ben's direction. 'I can't believe those two spent all night together in this tiny room, very cosy. They may as well have banged themselves up in one of the cells. I'd have gone mad. I wonder what they talked about.'

'Computer geeky stuff probably,' Julie said. 'Must be a buzz for them, something like this and more or less written permission to trawl the internet peering into anything they feel like.'

'What now then, boss?' Jack asked.

'Go and check on Spencer and Jefferies for me. They're working on the John Williams stuff, better make sure they're not killing each other.'

Jack wandered upstairs to the incident room and discovered the officers working quietly side by side, coffee cups at their elbows, the tabletop covered with neat piles of paper. On a nearby desk was a large cardboard box filled with photographs and other tatty looking documents.

'How's it going, lads?' Jack asked, pulling up a chair.

'Pretty slowly, Sarge,' Mark said. 'We've checked through John Williams' property lists, nothing of any interest, no drugs or anything associated with the scene. He doesn't appear to have a family. Mum and dad died when he was young and he was brought up in care. As far as we can see, his parents were only children and we haven't been able to discover any other family members.'

James dragged over the box. 'This is the stuff we found in his flat which might give us a clue to any contacts he had. Social Services told us he was fostered for a couple of weeks when he was in his teens, but it didn't work out and he returned to the children's home. Spent a little over ten years there, he was five when his folks died. Left the home when he reached sixteen. It was then he started nicking cars. A year in a young offender's institution, then, a couple of years later, a short spell in real prison for the same thing. It's a sad story.'

'Did he have a Facebook account?' Jack asked.

'He didn't have a computer,' Mark said.

'There are such things as internet cafes, Constable,' Jack said. 'He must have had some friends, someone who would be sorry to hear about his death. Surely no one lives entirely on their own these days. Get on with it and I'll check with you at the end of the day.' Jack stood.

'How's it going with the Consortium?' Mark asked. 'Any good news?'

'Still working on it,' Jack growled and left the room in search of coffee.

Chapter twenty-one

The colonel and the conspirator were alone in the chat room on the dark web, arguing heatedly.

'You must have some information for me!' the colonel raged, a poor connection made him sound like a monster. 'That's what we pay you for – information.'

'I can't tell you what I don't know, can I?'

'You need to make it your business to know.'

'You were tipped off about the surveillance on the pills. Don't forget how I saved your sorry ass. They'd have nicked you sure as anything.' The conspirator hesitated. 'I want out, OK?' he said. 'You've said yourself I'm not much use if I can't supply you with the goods and after all these months I've had enough.'

'That's tough, isn't it? You have no way out,' the colonel snapped. 'If this scheme collapses around our ears, you'll be dragged in as well, and your bosses will find out everything. Do you really want that?'

The conspirator remained silent.

'I thought not and it will all come out, you know that, don't you?'

'Yeah, I do know that.'

'Once the new lab is up and running, ready cash will make you feel better, but you must keep your ears to the ground. It's all very well knowing the police are planning something, but it's not much use without knowing what, so stop your pathetic whinging and do the job we pay you for. Who knows, if you outgrow your usefulness, your secret may slip out anyway and what are you going to do about it?'

'Are you threatening me?'

'Of course I am. You have no idea who I am. I can vanish. I have the money and the contacts. What do you have?'

The conspirator knew the colonel was right, and cut the connection angrily. He still had no choice and couldn't think he'd ever get out from beneath the enormous shadow he'd constructed for himself.

* * *

The cramped room in the bowels of the police station was quiet apart from the soft whirring of computer cooling fans. The available space had decreased steadily over the last few weeks as Ian and Todd brought in more and more equipment. Even so, entry into the Skype-like meetings still eluded them. Neither expert had been able to find a way in, although they were aware the Consortium had been communicating regularly.

A week ago, a detailed email from the colonel arrived providing the location of the new laboratory, an ex-workingman's club not far from Ammanford. The Colonel informed his new employee there was a flat attached to the empty building that he was more than welcome to use as part of the remuneration package. The £22,000 salary per annum offered seemed a touch on the high side, but nothing illegal had been discussed so far and Bitcoins hadn't been mentioned. The colonel signed off saying Darren would be contacted again nearer the start date.

Ian updated the small team.

'No luck with the live chat room, I'm afraid,' he said. 'The bottom line is until we're sent the rest of the encryption code, we can't gain access to what they're discussing. The site is busy, though, lots of meetings at all times of the day and night. The locations of the computers still aren't known and Todd has been chasing dead end IP addresses all over the world. In one of his emails to "Darren", the colonel states he's out of the country and could well be for all the information we've been able to uncover.' Ian flipped open a file and referred to his notes. 'Todd has decoded all the emailed correspondence using the section of the code we do have, and he's certain we're dealing with three men and one woman – the councillor. The modus operandi during the last recruitment is identical to our application. The councillor chats with candidates for a short while, then asks for a CV, part of a vetting process maybe. It's then that the colonel becomes involved; the chats are moved and the councillor takes no further part.'

Todd interrupted his friend. 'Something I find odd is that so far there has been no mention of anything dodgy. I mean, we're a week away from the start date and no one's said anything about making ecstasy. When they were buttering Cavendish up, the colonel was hinting at something only a week or so after the original contact.'

'Do you think they know we're listening and are playing us for idiots?' Jack asked.

'No idea. Maybe they're just being extra careful having already lost one chemist. They're bound to be nervous, surely, worried they might be discovered; that he talked.'

'Not if they killed him,' Julie said. 'He couldn't tell us anything after he'd died, could he? After Jeremy's death, we went to chat with John Williams and guess what? He died too. We can't put anyone on the ground until we know more about who we're dealing with, the whole thing is far too dangerous. The Consortium could be anyone and I'm afraid they've sussed us. All this stuff could be a trap.'

'Jack, are you still OK with it?' Ben asked. 'You're free to stand down, it's not a problem.'

'No, I'm still up for it.' Jack noticed a look of anger on Julie's face. 'As I see it, all I have to do is turn up at the lab looking like a mature chemistry student, settle in and start making pills. I can do all of that except the pill manufacture and I'm sure I can think up plenty of excuses why production isn't happening, and it's not like I'm going to be staying there for months, is it? I envisage a quick operation, maybe stay a couple of days, have a good sniff around undisturbed, then back here with the goods. Should be easy.'

Julie glared at him and stomped out of the room, pulling the door behind her with a clang which echoed loudly through the custody suite.

* * *

Ben and Jack sprawled on old, wooden deckchairs in the back garden of Stacey's cottage and shared a bottle of wine, too full to move far after a large meal, whilst the evening still held on to some summer warmth. Stacey and Julie wandered down to the far end of the garden and sat on the fence, gazing across open farmland, golden in the late evening sunshine. Stacey was concerned about her friend as she hadn't seemed herself over the last few weeks and during their recent telephone conversations, she became convinced Julie was keeping something from her. Julie was pale and had lost most of her bubbliness and Stacey couldn't remember when she last heard her laugh. Leaning closer she nudged Julie gently.

'What's up with you?' Stacey asked.

'Nothing. I'm fine.'

'I can tell you're not, haven't been for a while now.' Stacey linked her arm with Julie's. 'Can't you tell me what's bothering you? Your secrets are safe with me, they always are.'

Julie glanced over her shoulder at their partners sitting close to the cottage, deep in conversation, then back at the mountain.

'You really will have to keep this quiet,' she warned, 'if you don't I'll lose my job, but I must talk to someone or I'll go out of my mind.'

'It's something serious, isn't it?' Stacey asked. 'Spit it out, I promise not to tell a soul.'

'You can't even talk about this with Ben, do you understand? Can you do that – keep something secret from that man of yours?'

'If it's so important and you ask me to, of course I can. We're not a single entity, we still have our own minds.' Stacey smiled encouragingly.

Julie took a huge breath and lowered her voice. 'They are working on an undercover operation.'

'Ben and Jack?' Stacey was astonished.

Julie nodded. 'They've been stringing the colonel along for weeks now online. They brought in a hacker, a friend of Ian's, and the two of them have been more or less living together in Builth nick.'

'Gosh, I didn't know about any of this.'

'No, they are keeping everything very quiet. They invented a new recruit, a replacement chemist, and made up a CV to fit Jack, in case he had to meet any of them, as in actually be the new guy.' Julie stopped to breathe.

'Bloody hell,' Stacey muttered.

'Ben reckoned Jack was the best candidate, being a non-local and having worked for the drugs squad in London. Jack jumped at the chance and I was so… cross… he agreed without even talking to me about it. The operation is getting close now, the chemist is supposed to report for work in a week. I've tried talking to Jack, but he keeps telling me not to worry. Easy for him to say.' Julie sniffed, scrubbing her damp eyes with the heel of one hand.

'I had no idea. Ben hasn't said anything to me about this at all.'

'He can't. It's too sensitive and if he knew I was telling you, I'd be shot, or at the very least sacked. There's only five of us who know all the details and Charlie Ambrose – obviously. Thing is, Jack was worried at the start of the investigation we had an insider somewhere. He thinks the Consortium was tipped off about the surveillance of the original laboratory and that's why we didn't catch anyone collecting the goods.'

'I can see why he thinks that.'

'I'm terrified the group had something to do with the recent deaths of John and Jeremy. If that's true, we don't have a clue who we're dealing with or any understanding of how powerful they are. Jeremy was in custody, for God's sake, how the hell could they have got to him?' Julie started to cry, tears streaming down her face.

Stacey held her close. 'I don't think that's likely. There's bound to be a better explanation. You've been working yourself up into a state and should have talked to me before now.'

'I couldn't, and shouldn't be now,' Julie sobbed. 'I love Jack so much, it was dreadful when he was shot a while back. I don't want to go through anything like that again.'

'You know he can look after himself, don't you?' Stacey asked. 'They call him "The Jack Hammer" in the nicks. You should have seen him at the rave in June, wading in, fists flying, completely fearless.'

'I know and that's the trouble. He's not invincible, no one is and…' Julie seemed to run out of things to say.

'And what?'

Julie turned to face her friend, eyes full of fear.

'I'm pregnant,' she whispered.

'Wow! Does Jack know?'

Julie shook her head. 'No, and he mustn't, he can't, not until this undercover rubbish is out of the way.'

'You should tell him. Maybe he'll back out of this crazy idea.'

'And maybe he won't, and how would that make me feel? No, this has to stay with us; don't tell anyone, you promised, Stacey.'

'I won't. I'm glad you told me and you can talk to me any time, you know that. I'll always be here for you.'

Chapter twenty-two

Sam Jenkins almost snatched the open bottle of wine from the landlord at his usual lunchtime haunt in the centre of Brecon, and sploshed a good measure in his balloon-like glass.

'Where's this feature piece you've been promising me for weeks, Stacey? It better be good cos I haven't seen much coming out of you recently.'

'Work in progress. Things keep changing while police are working the ecstasy case.'

'So they are still working on it? I thought they'd given up, there's been nothing about it in the paper!' Sam glared at her.

Andrew Carr looked embarrassed and concentrated on cutting up his over-large steak, sure he'd never get through it all. He hoped the kitchen would give him a doggy bag.

'Your sarcasm's improving, boss.' Stacey took a long drink from her fruit juice. 'You don't want half a story, do you? I've already written the first section about the dance scene and a good chunk of the second, but don't you think it would be great to have an amazing ending, lives saved, bad guys caught, all that good stuff – the stuff that sells papers?'

Sam poured more wine and although he tried to hide it, Stacey spotted amusement in his eyes and knew he secretly enjoyed their verbal duelling.

'Of course it would,' he snapped, 'but in the meantime, we still have to fill the pages of *The Mid Wales Times*. If there's the chance of a good ending, make sure you're there when it happens. Get Ben to give you the heads up, you are the "People's Reporter" after all.'

'Don't fret, boss, I'm on it.' Stacey pushed away her empty plate and grinned. 'As I have so much time on my hands, is there anything you want me to cover?'

'Yes, I'm the boss and the only one allowed to be sarcastic!' Sam topped his glass up yet again, emptying the bottle. 'The Izzy Evans Trust has an event at the Bicycle Museum in Llandrindod one evening this week. Someone from a national drugs agency will be giving a talk and one of our local boys in blue is planning to attend. That'll be worth a couple of column inches, more if you can get me a decent photo to go with it.'

'What about me, Mr Jenkins?' Andrew asked.

'Thought we'd test you out with a touch of investigative reporting. I received a letter from a woman recently who is convinced an ex-neighbour has made off with funds collected for a local charity. Told me she tried to report the matter to the police, but they're not taking her very seriously and she doesn't want to let it drop. How about you go and have a dig around? We covered the main fundraising events last year, so check archives for the background story before you visit.' Sam held out a crinkled envelope. 'All the details are on there.'

Stacey thanked her boss for lunch and led the way out of the gloomy interior of the pub.

'How do you stand him?' Andrew asked. 'He's always so bloody grumpy.'

'Don't tell him I said so, but it's all a put-on. You shouldn't let him bother you, I reckon he reads lots of American novels in which the local newspaper editor is always grumpy and overbearing. It's all play-acting with Sam, anyway, he can't be that unimpressed or he wouldn't have given you an investigative assignment. I know for a fact he was impressed with your sleuthing at the rave.'

'Really? What did he say?'

Stacey giggled. 'This is Sam we're talking about, it's what he doesn't say that matters. If you need any advice give me a call, I'm always around. You'll have to come over to the cottage one evening, meet the gang.'

'The gang?'

'Me, my copper boyfriend, his sergeant – the one I told you to watch out for – and his partner: all useful contacts if you're planning on hanging around.'

* * *

DCI Ambrose leaned forward in his chair and examined an A4-sized photograph. Ben and Jack sat on the other side of the desk and waited.

'Is this the location of the new lab?' he asked.

Ben nodded. 'Jack and I went out for a discrete scout around and took these pictures. The place is a large, abandoned building about halfway between Brynamman and Ammanford, in the middle of a built-up area, lots of ex-miners' houses, sort of ribbon development which almost links the towns. There is a lot of cover for surveillance purposes. If DS Trent does go in, we'll have plenty of opportunity to keep an eye on him, and stop him getting into any trouble.' Ben grinned at his sergeant.

'This is a serious undertaking,' Charlie growled. 'I've been talking this over with the brass and they are only prepared to let it happen if we can demonstrate the risk to our officer is minimal. One thing in our favour is DS Trent has plenty of past experience with this sort of operation; he made a convincing busker in Brixton a while ago, I believe.'

Ben glanced at Jack who remained passive, his expression an unreadable blank.

'Run through everything again, will you?' Charlie asked and settled back in his chair, eyes half closed.

Ben cleared his throat. 'The new chemist is due to start on the 18th of this month – next Monday,' Ben said. 'He has been told in an email to report to the working men's club at ten in the morning, where he will be met by someone who will show him round the lab and living accommodation. The Consortium have made it quite clear that "Darren" is expected to run the lab single-handed.'

'Jack's just going to turn up then, is he?'

'More or less. We'll pack a car with enough stuff to make it look convincing and the computer wizards have been working on false ID documentation, utility bills, driving licence, that sort of stuff. We've arranged a mobile phone contract in Darren's name so if anyone should look, he'll have a digital footprint. The vehicle Jack will use is also in Darren's name, a logbook showing the previous English address in his belongings – on the rare chance anyone looks.'

'Good move. Continue.'

'We've managed to rent a storage room above a newsagents almost directly opposite the hall and will position a round-the-clock surveillance team there. Access is via an independent back door so it couldn't be better. There are a couple of shed-type buildings in the grounds of the actual hall, quite a large, stone-built one at the rear and we can tuck a couple of lads in there without being detected.'

'Is anything happening at the moment?' Charlie asked.

'Three visitors in the last week.' Ben rummaged around in the paperwork and handed over a few photos. 'This woman and two younger males. Bad pictures, taken on the move, but none of them have been near the place for the last three days.'

'I think they were there to set up the lab and living accommodation,' Jack said. 'Now that's done, all that's missing is their chemist.'

'But you're not one,' Charlie muttered. 'How are you going to convince them you are? Surely you have to know something about chemistry?'

'Constable Bradshaw has been coaching me for a couple of weeks – I can sound convincing, believe me.'

'What I find curious is they haven't yet mentioned anything about manufacturing illegal drugs,' Ben muttered. 'In the emails to Cavendish, they were pretty upfront about it; they told him they'd pay him in Bitcoins. There's been none of that in our communications with them.'

'They hadn't lost an employee before, they're just being super careful.' Jack smiled. 'It'll be fine, I can't understand why you're all getting so worked up. You'll be watching me all the time, I've got a phone and the chances are I won't see anyone at all. I wonder if they leave out a book of instructions or something. Shame we can't ask Jeremy.'

* * *

Jack opened the oven and removed a steaming leg of roast lamb, the gamey smell filled the kitchen and made his mouth water. He transferred the joint onto a china platter, surrounded it with golden potatoes and parsnips, and then called up the stairs.

'Come on, Jules, supper's ready. Are you still in the bath?'

'I'll be there now in a minute. Just finishing.'

Jack picked up an old carving knife and began cutting slices off the joint. Julie shuffled into the kitchen, dressed in a fluffy bathrobe and a pair of well-worn slippers.

Jack smiled at her. 'You look a picture, my love.' He leaned close to kiss her. 'And smell amazing, better than supper that's for sure. Hope you're hungry, the lump of meat your Da gave us is huge, he must have some monster sheep. It will take us days to get through, even if I eat lamb sandwiches for a week.'

Julie sat at the table, dragging fingers through her long hair to tease out the tangles. 'It looks lovely, *cariad.* You're turning into quite a chef on the quiet, aren't you?'

'Who'd have thought it?' Jack chuckled. 'I lived on takeaways in London, delivered to my door, so I got lazy I guess. Had to learn how to cook when I moved, haven't been able to find anyone who will bring me a pizza out here.' He handed his partner a glass of wine and placed a full plate in front of her. 'Dig in.'

Julie sipped the wine, belatedly remembered she shouldn't be drinking and started on her food. She wasn't very hungry and didn't know whether it was due to nervousness regarding the forthcoming operation, or because of the embryo growing inside her. She picked at her food, cutting small pieces of meat, chewing woodenly, forcing herself to swallow.

Jack noticed. 'What's up, love, not hungry?'

'Not really.'

'You're not still worrying about this undercover thing, are you?'

'Of course I am. How can I not worry about it? I wish you'd back out.'

'I can't, not this late in the game, everything's been set up and I'd be letting them all down.'

'Ben would understand, you know he would. We know nothing about this group of people, who they are, where they are, nothing. It's not safe, *cariad.* What if they killed the two boys to keep them quiet? If they suss you out they might shut you up too. I still can't believe you agreed to do this without talking it over with me.'

'And I've said I'm sorry. I honestly didn't think about it and have plenty of experience of this sort of caper. I've been undercover before in the smoke, spent three months masquerading as a busker on the mean streets of Brixton, grew corns on my arse from sitting on the pavement.' He chuckled and sipped from his glass. 'This should be a walk in the park compared to that, and Ben's covered everything as far as I can see. Officers will be watching the place all the time I'm there and it'll probably all be over in a couple of days at most. If we can nab just one of the Consortium, Ben thinks we can wheedle the names of the others out of him. It will be OK, love, I can look after myself.'

'Yeah, I heard – "The Jack Hammer".'

'What?'

'That's what they call you in the local nicks. Didn't you know?'

Jack chuckled. 'No I didn't, cheeky bastards.'

'It's not funny, Jack. I don't know what I'd do if anything happened to you.'

'Nothing is going to happen to me, the boss won't let it. He's been over everything with Charlie Ambrose and he's convinced it's safe.'

'What about the informer you've talked about ever since this case began? If you're right, you could be walking into a trap. The Consortium might be waiting for you and if they did kill those boys, getting rid of a copper won't bother them.'

Jack didn't know what to say and concentrated on his food. Julie picked at her supper a little while longer, then gave up.

'I'm sorry, really not hungry, no reflection on your cooking.'

'I'll have a word with Ben,' Jack said. 'I'll ask him to make sure you're involved in the surveillance. You'll see it's safe then and be able to keep an eye on me yourself. Please don't worry, sweetheart. In a couple of weeks it'll all be over and I promise not to accept any assignment like this in future without talking to you first.' He stood behind her, wrapped his thick arms round her body and hugged her tightly, surprised to realise she was crying.

Chapter twenty-three

The Consortium met in the dark web chat room.

'So we're set up then, everything in place?' the colonel asked.

'All done,' the cashier said. 'The lab has been commissioned and ready for use, and the flat has been stocked with supplies. I've run checks on Redfern and he seems clean. Does he know what he's going to be doing?'

'Not yet. I'm planning to send him instructions after he's settled in. I'm not predicting any problems though, everyone wants money, so I can't see him backing out when he discovers how much is on offer.'

'I hope not,' the councillor grumbled. 'We have to get up and running again soon or we're going to lose customers and we've put a lot of work into this over the last few weeks.'

'You worry too much,' the cashier said. 'If there was anything to worry about, we'd have heard. For God's sake, relax. The police don't seem to be making any inroads at all, so calm down and get ready to count your ill-gotten gains.'

'Who are you sending to meet Redfern on Monday?' the councillor asked.

'One of the guys who set up the lab,' the colonel answered. 'I've told him to wear a suit, make things look kosher and he's been well paid. The money makes him reliable and he wants more of it. We'll give the new chemist a couple of days to settle in and then, with a bit of luck, we'll be back to full-time production.'

* * *

Constable Spencer parked the car a couple of hundred yards down the road from the abandoned hall in Ammanford. Ben was growing increasingly nervous about the plan and wanted to check around the area again to search for any weak spots. Spencer was dressed in civvies and pleased to have been included on the mission. His association with the inspector couldn't do his career any harm at all.

'What now then, sir?' he asked.

'We'll sit for a while, see if there's any activity and if not, take a closer look. I want to check out the shed at the back of the hall. If there's a way we can get access to it without having to go in through the front, we can install a surveillance team during the night so they're in place ready for the eighteenth. The stockroom above the newsagents isn't a problem, has good rear access, but is a touch too far away for my liking. Be better if we could have some guys closer to hand – just in case anything goes wrong.'

After half an hour, Ben opened the door and climbed out. Spencer joined him on the wet pavement and turned up his collar against the dense drizzle.

'I bloody hate weather like this,' he grouched. 'Either rain or don't rain, this misty stuff is miserable.'

'Let's grab a cuppa in the greasy spoon next to the newsagents,' Ben suggested, 'good place to watch the hall for a while.'

Spencer led the way, held the door open for his boss and ordered drinks while Ben sat in the window seat brushing water off his jacket. The window was thick with condensation, opaque in places, but they'd be able to see if anyone approached the abandoned building. Spencer carried over two mugs and sat next to Ben who was squinting through the glass.

'It's a massive building,' Spencer said. 'The place they used before was tiny compared to this, I wonder why they picked here?'

'It's been closed for years. Ian checked with the local council and nothing has been done with it since the doors shut nearly ten years ago. Empty buildings are pretty much ignored these days, people forget they're there, so it's a good choice.' Ben drained his tea. 'Drink up, let's go and have a closer look.'

The men left the cafe, glancing up and down the street. It was deserted, not a single inhabitant prepared to brave the inclement weather. Ben led the way, crossed the road quickly and nipped up the side of the hall, trying not to brush against the undergrowth and soak his trousers.

The side path was very overgrown and in places brambles nearly blocked access completely. It appeared locals had been using the plot as an unofficial rubbish dump. Old furniture, empty paint cans and beer bottles were strewn about and the officers had to pick their way through the debris carefully. At the rear was a small patch of equally scruffy ground and a low shed squatted against the back wall. Making sure they were unobserved, Ben shoved open the wooden door, slipped inside, and waited for his eyes to adjust to the lower light level. The roof appeared to be intact apart from one corner where a drop of rain splashed into a puddle which was growing steadily beneath the leak.

'It's certainly big enough for our purposes and more or less watertight,' Ben said. 'We could stash a couple of lads in here and they would be invisible – unless of course someone actually came in, but the place doesn't look used. Find out if we can access it from the rear, Constable, make things much easier when we have to change shifts.'

Spencer left the shelter of the decrepit building and Ben heard him rummaging about behind the wall. Peering out of the single window, he saw he had a perfect view of one of the lower windows of the hall. A moth-eaten scrap of cloth covered the glass preventing him from actually seeing inside, but that was easily fixed. Jack could remove it when he was in, then they'd have a much better idea of what was going on inside. Spencer ducked back into the shed.

'No problem getting in through the back, sir,' he said. 'There are allotments on the other side of the wall, so we can come in that way. No one will be working their patch in the dark, so we shouldn't be spotted.'

'That's good news. Let's get back to the nick and make final preparations for Monday.'

* * *

As soon as they arrived at Builth station, Ben called a meeting in the incident room. He needed to recruit a reliable team for surveillance, available the entire time Jack was in the field. His sergeant's concerns about an informer were uppermost in Ben's mind, but an operation of this size needed backup and that meant more people being in the know.

The problem had bothered him for days now. He'd talked it over with Jack and they'd discussed likely candidates, settling on Julie Smith, Mark Jefferies, James Spencer and Ian Bradshaw, bolstered by four uniforms who were to be told as little as possible, as late as possible. Todd Morgan would continue to monitor chat rooms from the station. A rota had been drawn up to ensure round the clock cover for forty-eight hours, Ben couldn't see there would be any need for Jack to stay in the hall longer. If he hadn't been able to discover anything useful in two days, the chances were the information wasn't there to find.

The officers assembled in the room looked nervous and excited, Julie positively grey under the harsh strip lighting. Ben asked if she'd be better sitting this one out, but she shook her head determinedly and he was glad to have her on the team. DCI Ambrose made a brief appearance to offer support more than anything, and warn his officers to exercise caution while the operation was underway. When the meeting broke up, Ben called Jack to his side.

'What's with Julie?' he asked quietly. 'She doesn't seem keen about this.'

'She's not,' Jack muttered, 'anything but. I haven't been able to talk about the operation without upsetting her. I don't know what's the matter with her, it's not as though I haven't got support. I've tried telling her you won't let anything happen to me, but can't convince her. It's so bloody silly. I reckon this operation will all be over before it really starts.'

Chapter twenty-four

By 18th August, preparations for the undercover operation were almost complete. Jack's car had been packed and was parked behind the station, and surveillance was already in place, keeping watch on the working men's club. One team in the room above the newsagents, another sequestered in the scruffy shed at the rear of the building.

Todd had received an email from the colonel during the night, which confirmed "Darren" would be met at the hall by a representative from the organisation who would explain the job, show him round the living accommodation and presumably inform the replacement chemist of what he would actually be manufacturing. There had still been no mention of the illegal nature of the work on offer and that concerned everyone.

'How can the Consortium be sure Darren will agree to work for them when he realises what he's being asked to do?' Ben wondered out loud.

'They're banking on the lure of money,' Todd said. 'Cavendish amassed a fair stash of Bitcoins during the couple of months he worked for the gang. The promise of riches often encourages people to do things they wouldn't normally consider. I reckon they're being cagey, making sure everything's safe, much as we are.'

'And is it safe?' Ben asked.

Todd nodded. 'I'm sure we've covered all the bases, at least on the digital side of things. I've set up systems downstairs to let me know if there's any online chatter, and the links to our mobiles are still in place. Ian's in the room above the shop and has a laptop linked to the main system here, so I'm confident we'll hear if there's any trouble or if we get sussed out. There's an old payphone in the lobby of the hall and we've been working with BT to get it operational. DS Trent can always use that to contact us if his mobile is compromised.'

'You do seem to have everything well in hand. Good work, Todd. At least I don't have to worry about cyberspace.'

Jack entered the room not looking much like himself. He hadn't shaved in a week, a short, thick beard sprouted from his face and his usually well-groomed hair stuck up in all directions making him look as though he'd just left his bed. He'd swapped his usual smart suit for a T-shirt, a faded pair of black jeans and a baggy jumper was tied around his neck by the arms. A pair of dark framed glasses and a laptop bag hanging from his left shoulder completed the look. Ben struggled to recognise his sergeant.

'You should have gone on the stage,' Ben said. 'I think you're wasted here.'

'You approve then, boss?' Jack asked.

'You'll pass. Are you ready? Got everything you need? Any last minute worries?'

'Nope, all's well. Let's get on with it. You look after your end and let me worry about mine. I'll contact you as often as I can, but feel it's best if you assume everything's OK unless you hear otherwise. The less chatter the better, mobiles are easy to hack. I have no idea how long I'll have company when I first go in, so don't panic, just make sure the surveillance teams keep their minds on the job.'

He caught Julie's eye and was sure he saw a tear sparkling in the corner. As he left the room, he squeezed her shoulder and smiled, mouthing the words, 'Don't worry'.

* * *

The team hidden in the upstairs room of the newsagents watched DS Trent park his car just before ten o'clock on the main road outside the empty hall. They had been in place since before light and no one had gone near the building.

Jack hauled himself out of the car and stretched, gazing around as though he had just completed a long drive. Bending back into the car, he dragged out the laptop bag, hung it from his shoulder, locked the car, then crossed the road and entered the cafe. He emerged a couple of minutes later with a lidded polystyrene cup and perched on the low wall outside the hall to drink.

Five minutes later, a slate-grey MPV with heavily tinted windows pulled up behind Jack's rusty Vauxhall. A youngish man stepped out, dressed smartly in a tailored suit, and shiny, patent leather shoes; he had neat, short-cropped hair, and a diamond glinted in his left ear. The surveillance team watched intently as the man walked towards Jack. The pair shook hands and spoke for a while on the pavement, before the new arrival led the way to the front door of the hall, used a large set of keys to unlock and swung it open, gesturing for Jack to precede him. The door shut behind them.

Ben turned to Ian who was peering through a camera balanced on the windowsill. 'Get any pictures?'

'Yep, no problem. I'll send a couple of the best to the nick where they can work on identifying this guy and check his vehicle registration.'

'I wish we could see what was going on behind the door,' Ben mumbled.

* * *

Jack followed the suited man into the musty dimness of the long abandoned club. Just inside the door, an old BT phone hung on the wall surrounded by yellowed taxi cards stuck to the plaster.

'Is the phone working?' Jack asked.

The man shook his head. 'No, but the other services are connected.'

A pair of swing doors opened onto a large room filled with dusty tables and chairs. At one side was a bar; a few filthy glasses were stacked on shelves behind the serving area, empty bottles attached to optics providing an environment obviously perfect for spiders as large tangles of webs dangled from them all.

'Are you sure we're in the right place?' Jack asked. 'Doesn't look much like a laboratory to me.'

'The lab's in the back. Follow me and I'll show you around. How long did it take you to get here?'

'Best part of four hours from Redhill and that was without any traffic jams. Had a remarkably good run over from England, first time I've ever been over the new bridge. Followed the satnav all the way, though I thought it had led me astray when I pulled up here. This isn't what I expected at all. Who chose this place?'

The man shrugged. 'The board, I guess. They are working on incredibly commercially sensitive stuff, lots of companies would love to get their hands on our research, so they tuck their labs away. It's also cheaper than setting up in one of the cities.'

The man pushed open a door at the back of the hall, walked down a narrow corridor and into a side room. Jack followed and was astounded by what he saw. Scientific equipment covered every available surface, overhead lights glinting on glasswork and stainless steel.

'Wow! What a great space.' Jack wandered around making a point of examining the workstations, sinks, Bunsen burners and unopened cardboard boxes. He flipped the lid on one, rummaged about inside and pulled out a plastic tub full of an off-white powder. Popping the top he warily sniffed at the contents and discovered it was odourless. Replacing the tub, he wandered around the bench and opened a second box filled with plastic, zip-top bags; thousands of them.

'Come on,' the man said. 'You can look through all that stuff later. Let me show you the flat. I have another meeting in an hour, so can't hang about much longer.'

He left the room, walked further along the hall towards the back of the building, opened another door onto the bottom of a narrow, wooden staircase and started to climb, the risers creaking and groaning alarmingly. He unlocked a door at the top of the stairs and ducked his head under the low lintel.

Jack was pleasantly surprised. The compact living room was carpeted and fairly clean. A small television sat on a side table and a large window overlooked the backyard. Jack peered out, glanced at the shed and resisted the urge to wave at his watching colleagues.

'There's a kitchen and bathroom through there and a smaller bedroom. You can use the flat as long as you work here.' The man grinned. 'Part of the benefits package.'

Jack found the kitchen and opened the fridge expecting it to be empty, but was amazed to find it full of essentials, milk, butter, some vegetables, a pack of bacon, half a dozen eggs and a small loaf of bread. The man noticed his surprise.

'The company wanted to make you feel welcome,' he said. 'Saves you having to hunt around for stuff when you've just arrived. There's a portable gas fire in the bedroom and a spare canister in the hall.'

'Will someone from the company come to show me what I'm supposed to be doing in the lab?'

'Probably not. There are instruction manuals in one of the boxes which will tell you all you need to know, plus copies of previous research material and a copy of the terms and conditions you agreed to, just in case you need reminding how sensitive this project is. If you have any problems, there's a computer in the lab that will provide access to the boss. He expects you to use the next couple of days to settle in, read through the manuals, find your way around the lab and start work mid-week. Any questions?'

Jack smiled. 'Quite a few to be honest, but I'll do as you say and maybe I'll be able to answer them for myself. I must say, I've never worked anywhere like this before, always been part of a research team. Being the master of my own lab will be quite an experience. Do I need to check in with anyone each day?'

'It's not necessary. The colonel was impressed with your qualifications, but he's not a chemist and will rely on you to inform him of anything he needs to know.' The young man checked the time on his mobile phone.

'Sorry, Darren, got to be off or I'll be late for my next appointment. Nice to meet you.' He held out his hand and Jack shook it. The man dropped a set of keys on a table near the door and left the flat, clumping down the stairs, through the hall and out onto the street. Jack heard the front door bang shut and he was alone.

* * *

Ben and his team saw the man leave the building, climb in his car and drive away. His registration number had already been checked and unsurprisingly it was a rented vehicle. Todd was checking with the hire firm for any ID information they held, and Ian managed to snap a couple more pictures as the man drove away.

'I don't recognise that guy – do you?' Ben asked as his phone vibrated in his pocket. Digging it out he checked the screen and saw Jack's number.

'All OK?' he asked his sergeant.

'So far so good. Quick call only, until I can make sure I'm alone. Tell Julie I'm fine.'

* * *

Jack cut the connection, wandered downstairs past the lab, entered the main hall and made for the front door. He lifted the grimy receiver of the payphone, held it to his ear and was heartened to hear the comforting purr of a dialling tone. Next, he examined the Yale lock on the main door. It had locked automatically behind the Consortium's man, so Jack flicked on the deadlock and shot home two heavy bolts at the top and bottom. No one could get in that way now, even if they had a key. He instantly felt more secure knowing it was unlikely anyone could sneak up on him during the night.

Retracing his steps to the main hall, he scouted around, not really sure what he was looking for. He checked the bar area, searched for any monitoring equipment which may have been hidden there and found nothing. He didn't really expect to, nothing similar had been discovered at the previous lab. Old, Welsh language newspapers littered the floor, outdated cigarette packets were scattered around, a worn, greasy cap sat on a round table, and a pair of faded raincoats hung limply from a hat stand looking like anorexic ghosts. The whole place appeared trapped in the past. He played with beer pumps on the bar and was not surprised to find them corroded and unusable. In the right-hand corner of the main hall was a window covered by a scrap of disgustingly dusty material. He yanked it down, scattered spiders and dead flies and peered through the cloudy glass. He stared at the stone shed, but couldn't tell there was anyone inside – just as it should be.

He went to the lab and started poking about. Discovering two hefty ring binders labelled as Manual One and Manual Two, he carried both up to the flat to work his way through them. Might as well be comfy and a cup of coffee to think with was required.

* * *

The surveillance teams kept in contact with each other. Spencer and Julie were hidden in the shed and saw DS

Trent tug down the curtain covering the window. Training their binoculars on the glass, they were disappointed they couldn't see very far into the interior and as soon as Jack moved away, they lost sight of him.

Chapter twenty-five

Stacey had just finished washing up after supper when she heard a knock on the front door. Wiping her hands, she pulled the door open and was surprised to see Julie on the step, looking even paler than the last time they'd met.

'Hey, good to see you,' Stacey said. 'You OK?'

Julie shook her head and stepped into the hall.

'I hope you don't mind,' she said. 'I've been on stake-out since lunchtime and can't face going home to the cottage with Jack away.'

'Of course I don't mind. Have you eaten yet?'

'No. I'm not hungry. I like the idea of food, but I get it in my mouth and can't swallow.'

'Well, that can't go on,' Stacey said. 'You're supposed to be eating for two, not eating for no one. Go through to the kitchen and I'll make you something while you tell me how things are with you.'

Julie sat at the table and watched as Stacey began breaking eggs and mashing bananas.

'Please, don't go to a lot of trouble,' she said. 'I really don't have an appetite, can't think about food while I'm so worried about Jack. He went undercover this morning, was met by a young business-like chap who showed him round the place. Jack's there on his own now and apart from a quick call to say everything was OK, we've heard nothing from him.'

'That's good, surely?' Stacey asked as she beat eggs in a bowl, added the mashed banana, a sprinkling of cinnamon, a spoonful of dark tahini and beat some more. 'Where is this place, can you tell me?'

'I shouldn't, but…' Julie rubbed her eyes. 'There's an old working men's club outside Ammanford, huge barn of a place, been empty for years. A new lab has been constructed in the back. We've been watching the place for a while now, but since Jack went in we've got two teams there round-the-clock to make sure he's safe.'

'Seems like Ben has everything covered then. He really won't let anything happen to Jack, you know he won't.' Stacey poured the blended mixture into a hot, shallow pan and it sizzled loudly. Turning the heat down, she made a pot of tea and placed it in front of her friend. 'How long is Jack planning to stay?'

'Haven't a clue. As long as it takes, I guess. He has plenty of time to sniff about so I'm hoping he'll find some trace of these Consortium members quickly, then get the hell out and we can round them up. Nothing ever works like that though.' Julie sniffed. 'What are you cooking?'

'One of my famous banana pancakes, very satisfying and they taste good too, especially with wild wimberry jam on top.' Stacey checked the pan and skilfully flipped the concoction over to cook the other side. 'How are you feeling? Everything OK with the baby?'

'Physically I'm fine. Nearly three months pregnant and I should be blooming, isn't that the expression? I look in the mirror and see a dandelion about to go to seed, nothing blooming about me.' She sighed heavily. 'I've been stuck in a manky, damp shed all afternoon with a copper I barely know, staring at the window of the hall hoping for a glimpse of my man. I soon realised that was all I was looking for, nothing else, so I guess I'm not doing much of a job.'

'You'd notice anyone going in or out though, wouldn't you? There's no one who wants to keep Jack safe more than you.' Stacey slipped the browned pancake on a plate, added a spoonful of deep blue jam and placed it in front of her friend.

'Now, eat. Pregnant women do not go on diets!'

Julie picked up a fork and cut a tiny piece, reluctantly putting it in her mouth, smiling as the flavours reached her taste buds.

'See?' Stacey said. 'Told you it was good. Are you back on surveillance tomorrow?'

'Yes, if Jack's still inside, first thing.'

'Why don't you stay the night with me? It'll be better than going back to the cottage on your own and Ammanford's no further from here.'

'I'd like that, Stace, thanks. I was dreading going home to an empty house with nothing to do but worry.'

* * *

The conspirator was again sitting in his car on the Epynt Mountain, listening to rifle shots from one of the nearby military firing ranges. It was a little after midnight, the sky was clear and he stared at the wild land lit by white moonlight. A couple of rabbits hopped about between sleepy sheep and he heard a nightjar call at the edge of the forest lining the road. He gazed at the night sky, smiling briefly as he spotted the flash of a shooting star, neon blue against the blackness. He sighed heavily and rubbed his eyes with the back of his hand.

He'd run out of ideas. He had been sitting here for hours and still couldn't make his tired brain function properly. The colonel had been hassling the last few days and so far he'd ignored him, but couldn't do that forever. Either the group would come after him, or send his shameful secret out to all and sundry. He groaned. How could he have been so stupid? A seventeen-year-old girl was way too young for him, especially as she turned out to be only fifteen. He'd never been able to work out how the colonel had obtained pictures of them together, or even who the bloody man was, but it didn't matter. The pictures existed and he had no doubt that if he threatened the Consortium, or failed to live up to his side of the deal, the photos would appear on the internet within minutes, and life as he knew it would end.

He'd considered handing himself in, owning up – to everything – let justice take its course, but wasn't sure he would be safe in prison, Cavendish hadn't been. Since the first cook house had been raided, the conspirator had tried to discover who the members of the Consortium were. He hadn't had much luck as they'd covered their tracks incredibly well and every search he conducted led him to a dead end. Then, quite by chance he had stumbled over the identity of the councillor. He knew who she was, but still had no clue about who the others were. He had considered driving off a cliff, but when he reached the coast quickly discovered he didn't have enough balls. He was truly pathetic.

He climbed out of the car to stretch his legs and breathed in the cool mountain air. He did have useful information he could pass on to the colonel, but knew he shouldn't, the consequences would be too dreadful. If he didn't… more dreadful consequences. He must think of something, burying his head and staying offline wasn't going to work for much longer. He walked a little way from the car, spooking the rabbits that shot for cover, then had a glimmer of an idea. He closed his eyes and concentrated, trying to focus his mind. It was a good idea and with tweaking, he thought he'd be able to convince the colonel the information he passed over was good. The whole thing was escalating so quickly and he must stop it. If misleading the colonel was the only way to achieve that, then so be it. He had no choice.

He walked back to the car, cranked the engine and set off down the hill towards home. For the first time in weeks he felt as though he was in control.

Chapter twenty-six

Jack woke in the small single bed above the working men's hall and almost forgot where he was. He stared at the high ceiling and pulled consciousness towards him. He stretched under the duvet, his feet poked out from under the covers and dangled over the end of the mattress. He squinted at a small clock on the bedside table and was surprised to see it was after eight. Who'd have thought he would have slept so well under such strange circumstances?

He sat up, swung his legs out from under the covers, hauled himself off the low bed and shuffled into the kitchen. While coffee was brewing, he washed in the small bathroom, threw on his clothes, collected the heavy manuals from the sofa in the living room and dropped them on the kitchen table.

As he sipped coffee, he opened the binders and flicked aimlessly through the hundreds of pages. He'd been through them both, cover to cover, working long into the night, but hadn't been able to discover a single mention of anything other than the production of fat dispersal drugs. Jack didn't understand it. As far as he could tell – using the limited knowledge Ian Bradshaw had instilled in him –

there wasn't anything there. No mention of illegal activity at all. He'd already checked his email account and had not received any communication from the colonel.

Finishing his coffee and pouring a second, he wandered downstairs and into the well-equipped laboratory at the rear of the hall. Switching on the lights, he began opening cardboard boxes, slicing the parcel tape with a box cutter he'd found on one of the work surfaces. Inside most were plastic tubs with tight fitting lids and they all contained powdered chemicals. He dug deeper in the box and discovered a sheet of paper detailing the contents. He read the words Phosphatidylcholine and Phosphatide. He frowned, they meant nothing to him at all. Rummaging around in the other boxes he found no more pieces of paper. Checking the outside of the boxes he saw the address labels had all been removed, so no further clues there, and no return address.

He climbed the stairs back to the flat, settled in front of his laptop and searched the internet. After a few minutes, he discovered that the chemical names were associated with the production of Lecithin, a fat burning drug. Jack was confused. He had worked through both manuals cover to cover and only read information on fat-burning drugs and how to manufacture them, nothing about making ecstasy. The chemicals in the lab backed this up and it really did appear as though he was expected to churn this stuff out. He wished he could talk it over with Ben, but didn't want to make too many calls in case his phone was being monitored.

Sitting in front of the computer screen, he pondered his next move. A message pinged in. The colonel was online, and wanted to know how "Darren" was settling in and whether there were any problems. Jack composed a suitable reply, said everything was fine, he was checking the equipment in the lab, had read through the manuals and should be in a position to start production in the next couple of days.

Realising he was hungry, Jack returned to the kitchen and began cooking bacon for a sandwich and while the rashers hissed in the pan, he made a quick call to Ben to let him know things were fine. The bacon crisped nicely, Jack cut two thick doorstops of bread, loaded the still sizzling meat inside and wandered back downstairs to the main hall. He opened all the store cupboards and checked inside the other rooms and found nothing except remnants left over from the days when the club had been open. One cupboard contained piles of dusty old ledgers, records of membership and account books. In another, mouldy floor mops and brushes stood beside boxes of ancient dusters squatted by mice which had shredded the material and used the yellow strands to weave their nests. The smell was disgusting and Jack quickly slammed the door.

On the opposite side of the building from the lab, he found a locked door. His curiosity pricked, he collected the bunch of keys from the flat and spent a fruitless five minutes trying to find one which fit the lock. He knelt on dusty floorboards and tried to shine his torch through the keyhole, straining to see anything on the other side with no luck. Returning to the main hall, he searched behind the bar and found a large screwdriver, rusty and worn, but it would do. Back at the locked door, he slipped the metal blade in the gap close to the lock and used his strength to lever it against the door jamb. The resultant splintering was far too loud in the silence of the abandoned building. Jack glanced over his shoulder in a reflex action and then dragged open the door. Shining the torch inside he was disappointed to discover he had just broken into a coal hole. A sliver of light shone at the rear of the space and he realised there was an outside door, somewhere the coalman could deliver the coal without needing access to main building. He crossed the small room, tugged at the door and heard a chain rattle outside, but the door remained closed and was secure. One last look round the dirty black room, then he left, pulling the door shut behind him.

Jack was struggling to understand any of this, nothing made any sense. There must be something here to lead the police to the Consortium, but if there was, he hadn't found it yet, so must be looking in the wrong places. He went back to the lab and started searching again, he must have missed something.

* * *

Ben and Julie had taken the first shift and were already hidden in the room above the newsagents.

'I can't see the point to this, sir,' Julie said. 'We may as well have got a search warrant, gone in and tossed the place. I can't see why Jack needs to be in there at all.'

'You know why. We're trying to discover the identities of the Consortium members and haven't been able to track them online. I'm hoping there will be something in the hall which will provide a clue to who these people are, prevent them disappearing inside cyberspace. If we'd just busted the lab, they'd have set up somewhere else and it's imperative we stop them making more ecstasy.'

'They must read the papers, though. Surely they know their pills have been killing people.'

'Perhaps they don't care,' Ben said. 'I arrested a pusher a few years ago who was cutting speed with scouring powder, dreadful stuff. When I asked him why he used such a caustic cutting agent, he said – and I quote – "doesn't bother me what the kids shove up their noses, I don't use it". All these people care about is making money, not how they make it.'

'Jack can't have found anything or he'd have been out by now,' Julie said. 'How long are you expecting him to stay there?'

'Until we get a break. You can see for yourself, he's in no danger. We're watching all the entrances so if anyone goes in, we'll spot them. We just need to be patient.'

* * *

Members of the Consortium met online after the conspirator had contacted the group and told them he had new information. He had thought long and hard about what to say and was confident they'd accept his story.

'What have you got to tell us?' the colonel asked.

'The cops have employed a hacker who is trying to trace us online.'

'We know that,' the cashier snapped. 'You told us that weeks ago and we adjusted our conversations so they don't know what we're talking about and it's working. They still don't have a clue who we are. You said you have something new to tell us.'

'They've been able to work out the councillor is a woman and they're busy decoding our earlier conversations with Cavendish. Colonel, are you sure you didn't leave any clues online?'

'Of course I didn't! Don't forget, we've been at this longer than you have. The police won't be able to find anything that could lead them to us.'

'How do they know I'm a woman?' the councillor asked, sounding concerned.

'The hacker worked it out, from the words and turns of phrase you used when you were busy recruiting.'

'Can they track me? Find out who I am?'

'If they could, they would have by now. They're talking about an undercover operation, putting one of their own in the field.'

The group fell silent, thinking about what the conspirator had said and the possible implications.

'How would they do that?' the cashier asked. 'Put a copper on the streets to get in with the dealers or what? I can't see that working. We'd know if a new face appeared and anyway, I know most of the local coppers by sight.'

'Not sure yet, everything's being kept very quiet, but we must be extra careful and no more contact using email –

they've broken the encryption and can read anything we send to each other.'

'Impossible!' the colonel spluttered. 'There's no way they could break the code, not a chance.'

'And I'm telling you they have,' the conspirator snapped. 'They are busy working on the contacts we had with Cavendish and it's that correspondence which has led them to the conclusion that the councillor is female. So far, they haven't been able to get into these conversations, so we are still secure as long as we use this method.'

'You need to find out more about this undercover operation they're planning,' the colonel said. 'Maybe you're just winding us up, passing duff information to get yourself off the hook, is that what you're doing?'

'Of course not! Just relax all of you, for God's sake. We're still safe and I want it to stay that way. Just be careful, that's all I'm saying and as soon as I know more, I'll tell you.'

The conspirator broke the connection, leaving the remainder of the group to argue between themselves. He'd bought himself some time at least, time to think about how he was going to get out of the bloody great hole he'd been digging himself during the last few months. There had to be a way.

Chapter twenty-seven

Stacey sat at the computer in her office at the cottage and switched it on. She called up the feature she was working on and began to read through what she'd written over the last weeks, but her mind was elsewhere. She couldn't concentrate on anything this morning, brain trapped in a bubble of worry and disturbing thoughts. She hadn't been able to settle at anything since Julie stayed a couple of nights ago, and wondered how her friend was coping. A baby should bring wonderful, exciting times, not this feeling of dread which perched on the back of her neck and made it difficult to breathe properly. The gang should be celebrating, not even acknowledging such good news was all wrong.

Ben still hadn't said anything to her about the operation underway and remained vague and distant when Stacey tried to question him, so she'd given up, and that was wrong too. They'd always been so close and now it felt like a barrier had been built between them, and she hated it. She understood he couldn't tell her everything about his work, but surely he knew she could keep his secrets. Unwelcome thoughts wriggled about in her grey matter and asked unpleasant questions, tried to suggest Ben was keeping other things from her, and maybe he'd not been open from the start of their relationship. Her heart told her otherwise, but the niggling inner voice would not shut up.

Again she tried to concentrate on the screen in front of her, but words floated around and made no sense.

'This is rubbish!' she said out loud, slapped the laptop shut, stomped through the kitchen and out to the damp garden. Even the weather was depressing, some sunshine would help, but it just kept on raining. She noticed she hadn't put the hammock away and a shallow puddle had gathered in the fabric. She tipped the canvas upside down to let the water sloosh out – and had an idea.

Returning to the kitchen, she put the kettle on, picked up the phone, dialled Andrew Carr's number and waited for him to pick up.

'Hi, Stacey. What can I do for you?' he asked.

'Are you busy at the moment?'

'Nope. Nothing until later, got to cover another meeting the Izzy Evans Trust is holding in town this evening. Can I help you with something?'

'I'm at a bit of a loose end myself, can't seem to get my head in gear and thought a drive might help. I wondered if you wanted to come with me, a sort of guided tour of the rest of your patch. You up for it? I'll pack a picnic.'

'Sounds like a great idea. Shall I meet you at your place?'

'No need. I'll pick you up in town in about an hour, is that OK?'

'Fine with me. I'll be ready.'

* * *

Stacey pulled up next to the large bronze statue of a red kite which dominated the tiny garden next to the bridge in Llanwrtyd Wells. A couple of minutes later, the back door opened, Andrew dumped a bag on the seat, slammed the door and slid into the passenger seat, smiling at his colleague.

'Where are we going?' he asked.

'I'm going to show you the whole of Wales.'

'What, all of it? Gonna be on the road a while then,' he said.

'I'm going to take you to the best view in the world from the Black Mountain. I hope the rain clears or it will be an utter disappointment.'

'The local weatherman said the sun would be out by lunchtime, so we might be lucky.' Andrew fiddled with his seat belt as Stacey pulled onto the main road.

She drove carefully on the twisty A483 and kept her eyes on the tarmac while her companion gazed out of the window at the passing countryside. They soon reached the main road at Llandovery, Stacey turned right and headed towards Carmarthen before turning off onto a smaller road. After they'd passed through Llangadog, the road became narrower and houses rarer. In the distance Andrew could see a craggy mountain rising into the clouds, the top completely obscured by the opaque murk of low clouds.

The car rattled over a cattle grid and as it began to climb up the hill, a burst of sunshine appeared from behind a cloud. Stacey concentrated on the looping road and watched for sheep straying onto the metalled surface. A cottage on the right of the road caught Andrew's attention.

'Wow! What a place to live,' he exclaimed. 'I'd love a house like that.'

'It's alright in the summer,' Stacey said, 'but winter is another matter altogether. The road is closed for weeks at a time when the snow comes.'

'Be OK if you stocked up,' Andrew said. 'The peace and quiet appeals to me. I could turn author and write novels instead of busting my arse for that ungrateful, grumpy sod in Brecon. He keeps on at me all the time, never gives me a break.'

'You should be grateful, Whippersnapper.' Stacey grinned at him. 'He's teaching you a trade. Taught me everything I know. "The Sam Jenkins School of Journalism" is – in my humble opinion – the best there is. Hang in there, if he didn't think you were worth the effort, you'd already be gone.'

The higher they climbed, the better the weather became and by the time they reached the top of the mountain road, the sun was shining brightly, burning away the thin cloud. Stacey pulled in at an empty viewing point and parked the car facing the way they had come. An incredible view spread out in front of them and Andrew had to admit it did seem as though the whole of Wales was laid out before him.

'This is absolutely stunning.' He climbed out of the car, pulled a compact pair of binoculars from his pocket and scanned the hills. 'The countryside is so empty, I can't see any of the towns and only a few farms. Look at that one in the middle of that patch of forest, wonderful! You'd never know it was there from lower down.'

Stacey opened the boot, dragged out a couple of folding chairs, a table and her wicker picnic basket. Andrew put down the binoculars and gave her a hand.

'Where does this road lead?' he asked.

'There's another five miles or so across the hills, then it drops down into Brynamman, onto Ammanford and back to Llandovery through Llandeilo. This is one of my favourite circular drives and lovely on a weekday, much quieter than at the weekend when heaps of people stream up here for hill walking.'

They had nearly finished their meal when another car pulled into the parking area and a family climbed out. Two young children galloped off over the grass, chasing a large black dog which ran around in circles, barking madly. The sheep grazing nearby scattered and Andrew frowned.

'I was just getting used to the peace and quiet,' he grumbled. 'Let's go, Stace.'

They packed the gear back in the boot and Stacey manoeuvred the car through the tight exit and back to the road. She drove slowly and as they travelled across the high plateau, a group of scruffy ponies sauntered onto the tarmac. They were stocky, hill animals, thick coats tufted, manes twisted with vegetation, with round bellies and sturdy legs. A couple of the mares had foals at hoof and Andrew insisted they pulled over so he could take some photos. Stacey watched him through the windscreen and smiled, his delight evident.

Leaving the mountain behind, they dropped down into Brynamman and the open views were replaced by terraces of grey houses, corner shops and several empty business properties. The small town was run down in places, a few empty houses boarded up and hardly anyone on the street. Stacey took her time, hunting for the abandoned hall. Andrew chatted away beside her, asking questions about mountain ponies and her answers became shorter as she concentrated on spotting the building. A mile or two further, on top of a slight rise, she found what she was looking for, slowed down and stared at the place through the side window.

Andrew noticed and peered past her. 'What's that place?'

'An old working men's club,' she told him. 'There used to be hundreds of these right across Wales when the pits were open. They were like community centres are today, but with many more members. A few years ago this was a thriving community, with iron and tin works as well as the mines. Clubs like this would be packed at the weekends with dances, local bands and male voice choirs. Sad to see these places empty now and no work in the area.'

'And we're interested in it because?'

Andrew's question came out of left-field and Stacey struggled to come up with a suitable response. She mumbled something unconvincing – even to herself – about a future piece and sped up, driving through

Ammanford towards Llandeilo. She'd forgotten how sharp her new colleague was and made a note-to-self to be more careful in future. She wasn't even sure why she'd felt the need to come and see the place for herself, let alone why she had brought Andrew with her. She really wanted to know what was happening with the police operation, wondering briefly if Ben was watching the place and whether he'd spotted her drive by. She hoped not, it would only make things more difficult and wished again they'd been able to talk to each other.

Chapter twenty-eight

The doorbell shattered the conspirator's thought processes and shocked him back to the present. He struggled out of the sofa and opened the door to see one of the local van delivery men standing outside.

He smiled. 'Hi, Phil. How's it going?'

'Not bad mate, thanks. Parcel for you.' The man held out a smallish, heavy box, collected the required signature, then hurried back to his van.

Puzzled because he hadn't ordered anything, the conspirator carried the package into the living room. Picking away the tape, he peeled it off in strips, then flipped the lid open. Inside was a white envelope, unaddressed, resting on a bundle wrapped in wadding. Unwrapping the material, he was horrified to discover it contained a small, vicious looking handgun and a rusted key. He dropped the objects on the coffee table and with shaking hands opened the envelope. A photo slipped out from between the folded paper and he glanced at it, already knowing what it showed, proof of his stupid indiscretion. He focused on the typewritten letter.

I know what has been going on. I know we have an undercover cop in our midst. What I don't know is why you didn't tell me, especially as you have so much to lose. Have you forgotten how much shit is waiting for you if you don't play by the rules, and how your shit pile has grown? Smuggling pills into police cells, making dodgy phone calls, shutting Williams' mouth for him. You have one chance – and only one – to make this right and save your sorry skin. You need to prove your loyalty to the Consortium, that you're on our side, because we are beginning to doubt you. This is your only chance – go to the hall and kill the copper – tonight. If he is alive in the morning, your life is over – one way or another. The key will get you into the hall via the coal hole.

The Colonel

'No, no, no.' The man threw the letter away from him and buried his head in his hands.

What the hell could he do? He started to sob hot selfish tears before realising they weren't going to help. He looked at the gun resting on the low table, reached out and picked it up. It was cold and heavy. He automatically checked to see if the safety catch was on and whether the thing was loaded. It wasn't, so he opened the box and discovered a clip of ammunition which he slid into the pistol's grip. Flicking off the safety, he held the barrel beneath his chin, hand shaking so badly he used both. He concentrated hard, sent mental commands to his right thumb to pull the trigger, but his body disobeyed and the digit refused to move. It was no good, he couldn't do it. He tossed the gun on a nearby easy chair and lay on the sofa while the world whirled around him, making him nauseous. He dashed for the bathroom just in time and clung to the toilet bowl, waiting for the spasms to subside.

Hours passed and the next time he looked at his watch, he saw it was nearly midnight. He felt terrible and couldn't see a way out of the hell he was in. The only thing he could think of was to go to the hall, take the undercover cop hostage, convince him he was going to be killed and hope he called in the cavalry who would – with a bit of luck – shoot him. All he wanted now was to die, couldn't do the deed himself, but was sure with the right encouragement, the police would do it for him. Suicide by cop.

He changed his clothes, dressing in black trousers with a dark hooded top, laced up his boots and went out to the car. He placed the loaded gun on the passenger seat, covered it with a book of maps and set off towards Ammanford on dark, empty roads. He found it strange that since he'd made up his mind he was going to die soon, life seemed so much easier. A kind of peace settled in his chest and he breathed easier than he had in months. A little over an hour later, he pulled to a stop on the outskirts of Lower Brynamman. The hall was still a mile or so away, but he knew how to get in from the rear of the property.

Leaving the road, he padded down a footpath which ran along the backs of terraced houses in the direction of the hall. One or two upstairs windows flickered blue as sleepy householders watched television in bed, but mostly the houses were dark. He walked quickly, ears alert for sounds, eyes peering through the dark watching for any movement, but saw nothing. Within twenty minutes he had entered the allotment site. He knew he couldn't go over the back wall as he'd be spotted by the surveillance team in the shed, so turned left, climbed over a low garden fence and headed for the side of the hall. About halfway along the building was the old coal hole, conveniently screened by a mass of brambles. He peered at the stone shed and listened carefully. There were no signs he had been detected, so he took the key the colonel had sent him out of his pocket, and inserted it in the padlock. It turned easily. He crept inside and quickly pulled the door closed behind him.

* * *

In the upstairs flat, DS Jack Trent snored gently in his sleep, oblivious that an uninvited guest was prowling around downstairs. Over the last couple of days, he had searched every box in the lab and found nothing at all to connect the hall with the ecstasy case. He had discovered no hard evidence of anything illegal and nothing to help the police identify the members of the Consortium. None of the chemicals were banned substances and, as far as he could tell, would only be useful in making fat busting substances. He reckoned the whole thing was a massive wind-up and had decided to draw stumps on the operation in the morning, it was just an enormous waste of manpower.

Jack snored on as the conspirator crept around the empty hall. He hadn't been inside before and was unsure of the layout. He dragged the gun out of his pocket and held it in front of him, but heard nothing. The copper was sure to be asleep, but the conspirator needed to check. As he crossed the main room his hip nudged a chair, the legs squealed on wooden boards and the man froze, listening hard. He heard nothing and moved slowly towards the bar, straining his eyes in almost total darkness.

Jack stirred in his sleep then was suddenly wide awake. He had no idea what had disturbed him, but lay motionless in the dark and listened. Hearing a soft noise from downstairs, he sat up slowly and crept towards the stairs. Standing at the top of the flight he wondered how he could descend the creaky steps without making a sound, when he spotted a shadow slide across the bottom step. Jack retreated to the flat and waited next to the door, back against the wall, barely breathing, heart pounding. After a few minutes, he heard a creak of protest from the stairs, judged his intruder was nearly at the top and focused his attention on the doorway.

* * *

Julie had volunteered for a second shift, unable to rest while Jack was working undercover. She squinted through the window of the storeroom of the shop and yawned. She rubbed her eyes, poured half a cup of coffee from the flask on the table and hoped the caffeine would wake her up. Looking back out of the window she thought she saw movement by the side of the hall.

'Boss,' she hissed. 'I think I saw something, come and look.'

Ben crossed the room to stand by her side and peered into the darkness.

'Where am I looking?' he whispered.

'Right hand side of the hall, about halfway back. I'm sure I saw something moving in front of the brambles.'

'Perhaps it was a cat, stray dog, fox maybe.'

'No, bigger than that. There! Did you see that?'

'See what?'

'Flash of a reflected street light.'

Ben took the night-vision binoculars from her hands and focused them on the side of the hall. In front of a dense bramble patch he spotted a low door standing ajar and frowned, he couldn't remember seeing the entrance when he'd scouted about last week.

'There's a door there,' he muttered. 'Looks like it's standing open.'

'We've got to go over, boss, now!'

'OK, take it steady, can't go rushing in without knowing what we're dealing with. Give me a couple of minutes to arrange backup.'

Ben worked the phone while Julie watched the hall anxiously, but saw no further movement. She wished Ben would get a move on, convinced her partner was in danger, and wanted to be there to help him.

* * *

The conspirator tiptoed into the flat and paused just inside the door to get his bearings. The place was dark, so he guessed the copper would be asleep in the bedroom. All he needed to do now was wake him up. He took another step forward and was suddenly hit by a dead weight, as though someone had thrown a bag of coal at him. He staggered backwards, hands scrabbled for the door frame, missed and he tumbled backwards down the flight of stairs, the weight falling with him.

Jack plunged down the staircase with the intruder beneath him and both landed heavily at the bottom, air punched from their lungs. The lighter man struggled furiously and managed to wriggle away from Jack, who scrabbled to his feet and made after him. As the prowler ran through the corridor and into the main room, Jack launched himself in the air, performed a graceless rugby tackle and brought his target down, hitting the floorboards with a heavy thump. Jack wrestled with the man, trying to flip him over and pin down his arms… the sudden gunshot was deafening.

* * *

Ben, Julie and Ian were creeping along the side wall, keeping to the shadows when they heard the shot. Julie pushed past the others, ignored her boss and yanked open the door. Finding herself in an old coal hole, she switched on her torch and frantically shone the beam around the walls looking for a way into the hall. The light illuminated old wood. Ben dashed ahead of her and barrelled through the door, shoulder first, yelling, 'Armed Police! Guns down! Show me your hands!'

Ian shone a powerful, handheld spotlight into the large open space and the beam settled on a mound of what appeared to be old clothes. Julie screamed. A heart splintering cry which echoed and re-echoed around the cavernous room. Ben grasped her arm, tried to hold her back, but she tore away from his grip and ran to the prone bodies, pulled at them, terrified what she might find.

One of the bodies groaned and stirred, the other was still. Ben tried to drag Julie away, but she clung on, shrugged his hands away, tugged at an arm and wailed. The front door flew open with a crash as reinforcements arrived and overhead fluorescents flickered into life, flooding the area with white light. One of the men on the floor moved, rolled away from the other, groaned again and said, 'Shush now, Julie love. I'm fine.'

'Jack!' She flung herself at him and he pulled her onto his lap, rocked her gently, arms clasped round her trembling body.

'There, there now,' he said. 'Don't carry on so. You're supposed to be a professional, what will the others think?'

Ben nudged the body with his foot, turned it over and was stunned to see Mark Jefferies looking up at him, still holding the gun. Ben wrenched the weapon away, flicked on the safety and handed it to Ian before kneeling by his constable's side. There was a large patch of blood below Mark's ribcage which was growing steadily. Mark groaned again.

'What the…?' Ben couldn't trust what his eyes were telling him.

Ian glanced down. 'Bloody hell, that's Mark, what's he doing here?'

'Your guess is as good as mine,' Ben said. 'He's taken a bullet in his stomach, whistle up an ambulance and tell them to make it quick. This looks bad.'

Ian made the call as Ben gently tapped Mark's face until the fallen man's eyes flickered open.

'Mark, what's going on? What are you doing here?'

'Told to be,' he wheezed, then coughed and groaned. His head lolled to one side and Ben shook him gently.

'By whom? Who told you? Constable, look at me!'

Mark gazed up, tears formed in the corners of his eyes, his body twisted in pain and more blood leaked onto the dusty floor.

'Colonel… sent me gun… said to kill…' He clenched his teeth against the pain.

'I don't understand, you're not making any sense.'

Ian stood by his inspector's side, wincing as Mark's body spasmed and the man whined in agony.

'Sorry, boss… had me by the balls. I'm the conspirator, I told them…' Mark spluttered and a thread of bright blood ran from the corner of his mouth. 'Had no choice.'

'Give me a name. Who is the colonel?'

'Don't know, only one… Hammond, Gwen.' His head slipped from Ben's hand and his eyes closed.

A commotion at the back of the hall announced the arrival of paramedics. Mark was lifted quickly but carefully onto a stretcher and rushed out to the waiting ambulance before being driven away at speed, lights flashing.

Ben glanced at Jack who was still cuddling a sobbing Julie.

'You OK, Sergeant?'

'Fine, boss. Nothing broken.'

'Did you hear what Mark said, admitted he was the conspirator?'

Jack nodded. 'Will he be OK, do you think?'

'Don't know. Does the name Hammond mean anything to you?'

'The orchid woman,' Julie mumbled. 'Jeremy's auntie.'

'Of course! What the hell can Gwen Hammond have to do with this?'

'Only one way to find out, boss,' Jack said, gently lifting Julie from his lap and hauling himself upright. There was a deep cut on one of his eyebrows, his lip had split and blood smeared his chin. 'Let's go and ask her.'

'I want to come,' Julie said. 'I'm not letting you out of my sight. Is that OK, sir?'

'Fine with me,' Ben said. 'Ian bring a car round, we can leave the troops here to keep an eye on this place, four of us will be plenty.'

Julie nipped off, used one of the sinks in the lab to wash her face and made a quick phone call on her mobile.

As soon as she heard Stacey's sleepy mumble, she hissed, 'Wake up! Get to the hall now and I never called.' She hung up and ran out to the waiting car.

Chapter twenty-nine

Ian stamped on the brakes and brought the car to an abrupt halt outside Gwen Hammond's home. The officers leapt out of the car, Jack reached the front door ahead of the others and pounded on it with a clenched fist, while Julie leant on the bell push.

They heard footsteps in the hall and as soon as the door cracked open, Jack yelled, 'Police!' and shouldered his way in, snapping the safety chain.

Gwen Hammond screamed in surprise and horror when she saw his bruised and bloodied face. Ben followed him into the hall, grasped Gwen by the arm, propelled her into the living room and pushed her on a chair.

'What's going on?' she asked.

'We want a word with you, several in fact,' Ben growled.

'But why come here in the middle of the night? Can't this wait until the morning?'

'No, it can't. What do you know about the Consortium?'

Gwen flushed red. 'What? Nothing! What are you talking about? What's wrong with him?' she mumbled and nodded towards Jack.

'Someone tried to shoot me, that's what's wrong with me,' Jack snapped. 'Now answer the inspector's questions.'

'I don't know anything about this and haven't a clue what you're talking about. Now get out of my house.' The dumpy woman tried to mask her fear with bluster and failed.

'We need you to tell us what you know about the Consortium.' Ben persisted.

'I've told you, I don't know what you're talking about.'

'Sorry,' Jack said, 'we don't believe you. You're coming to the station and we'll interview you formally there. Julie, get her dressed, I'll be out in the car.' He stormed out of the room.

Ten minutes later, the car pulled away from the kerb and Ian drove towards Builth Wells police station. No one spoke apart from Gwen who constantly protested her innocence.

* * *

Stacey parked her car a couple of hundred metres away from the abandoned hall and peered through the windscreen. She counted at least five police cars and a group of uniformed officers standing on the pavement in a dense group. From her position, she heard the static crackle of radios and subdued conversation, while blue lights bounced off buildings on each side of the road. Several sets of curtains had twitchers behind watching the action through the gaps, and blue and white police tape fluttered in the night breeze, strung across the entrance to the hall like an enormous game of cat's cradle.

No one had noticed her arrive and she took advantage, pointed her camera in their direction and shot a good crop of pictures before leaving the car. She walked along the opposite pavement and took another clutch of photos before crossing the road. She was soon spotted and James Spencer strode towards her.

'Ms Logan. Can I help you?' he asked politely.

'What's happening?' she asked.

'Nothing I can tell you about.'

'All these coppers, I didn't know Dyfed Powys Police had so many, must be something big, can't you tell me anything?'

'No, I can't, I'll get into bother. How is it that you're here?'

'Had a tip off something was going on,' Stacey said vaguely. 'Go on, officer, give me a clue. I won't quote you.'

'No chance. You're gonna have to leave.'

'Sorry, Constable, but I'm not going until you tell me something. DI James is my partner – you know that – and I'm worried about him. He's not answering his phone, so I'm going to sit here and watch unless you tell me I have nothing to worry about.'

Stacey settled herself on a low garden wall and pulled her jacket together to keep out the damp of early morning, camera in her hand.

Spencer groaned. 'You mean it, don't you?'

Stacey nodded. 'I do, and don't think you can force me to leave, I can be very determined.'

'So I've heard,' Spencer grumbled, although the hint of a smile lifted the corners of his mouth. He leaned in closer. 'OK, but I never said anything. Don't let me down, you could get me the sack if the boss knows I've spoken to you.'

'I promise. If there's a story, I'll write it – it's my job after all – but I promise I won't attribute anything to you.'

'There's been a shooting,' he whispered.

Stacey gasped. 'Who's been shot?'

Spencer glanced over his shoulder at the gang of officers on the opposite side of the road, but none of them were paying any attention to him.

'If I tell you, you have got to go.'

Stacey nodded and stared directly into his eyes.

'One of ours,' he hissed.

'Oh God! Not DS Trent surely? Tell me he's OK.'

'He's fine. It was DC Mark Jefferies. He's been taken to hospital, but it doesn't look good.'

'Bloody hell! How did it happen?'

'Don't really know ourselves yet, so you'll have to content yourself with that. Now, get shifted. Keep your side of the deal.'

'Where are the others? Are they OK?'

'If by "others" you mean DI James, DS Trent and DC Smith – they're not here. They were, but they've gone. We're only here to protect the crime scene until SOCO arrive. Now, get back in your car and leave. I won't tell you again and if you don't go, I'll nick you for obstruction and we'll take you to the station.'

Stacey started to protest.

'I know it's not fair, but this is a serious investigation. We don't want the press hanging around and getting in the way, so move yourself. Best I can do, sorry.'

Stacey could tell he meant what he said so shrugged her shoulders and strolled back to her car. She drove slowly past the hall and took a last look. As soon as she was out of sight, she pulled the car into a gateway, dug out her mobile and called Andrew Carr. His phone rang a couple of times before it was answered.

'Andrew, it's me, Stacey.'

'Bloody hell, what time is it? Sun's not up yet, what do you want?'

'Listen carefully. A story is unfolding and I need your help.'

Andrew coughed. 'OK, I'm awake, tell me.'

'Do you remember the hall we looked at the other day, the one on the edge of Ammanford?'

'Yep, what about it?'

'There's been a shooting there, a copper's been shot and has been taken to hospital. I'm off to track him down, but the police are still at the hall. I couldn't get very close before they suggested I leave. Any chance you can drive over and keep an eye on things for me? I've got a few photos, but they're not wonderful. I'll need something better to go with the words. Make sure they don't spot you, they'll move you on if they do. At least they don't know who you are, that should make things easier.'

'Wow! A proper story. I'm on it, Stace, thanks.'

'This is my story don't forget, so no poaching. You're going there to assist, not take over.'

'Don't worry, I won't. Keep in touch though, won't you?'

'I'll call you from the hospital once I've tracked down the victim.'

Stacey broke the connection, restarted the car and set off towards Cardiff, taking a gamble the hospital there was the most likely around to be able to treat a gunshot wound.

Chapter thirty

Gwen Hammond had refused to be interviewed until her solicitor was present so the officers waited together in the large incident room, drinking coffee and planning their next moves. Jack had been cleaned up by the station doctor and dosed himself with extra strength painkillers. His head was pounding and he'd pinched a nerve in his back when he fell which was sharply painful. He winced each time he took a breath.

Ben noticed his discomfort. 'Are you sure you wouldn't be better off at home?' he asked his sergeant.

Jack shook his head.

'No chance, boss, I'm not missing this bit for anything. I'm fine and the doc agrees, just a bit stiff here and there. I only fell downstairs, haven't been shot like Jefferies.'

'We need to know why he was there,' Julie said, 'and we have to search his place. It's not like we can ask him anything, but maybe we'll find something at his flat to explain all this.'

'I hope so,' Ben muttered. 'I can't understand why he'd be involved with the Consortium, yet he told me he was the conspirator, said the colonel had ordered him to go to the hall and shoot Jack. Why the hell would Mark agree to do a thing like that?'

'Julie's right, boss.' Jack drained the last of his coffee and dragged himself to his feet. 'Constable Bradshaw, go and find a car, we'll go over now. See if you can round up someone from SOCO, in case we need them.'

* * *

Stacey collected another coffee from a vending machine in the corridor and wandered back towards the waiting room outside Cardiff Hospital's Intensive Care Unit. The wards were quiet, the only sounds the whirr and bleep of monitoring equipment and the squeaky, shuffling footsteps of medical staff. Unsurprisingly, Mark was in a high dependency ward, connected to a whole wall of machines and not receiving visitors. A uniformed police officer sat uncomfortably on a plastic chair in the corridor outside the room and glanced up as Stacey walked by. On impulse, Stacey offered the man her coffee and he smiled.

'I can't take your drink,' he said.

'I could go and fetch you one if you like.'

'Would you? That would be great. Milk and sugar please.'

A couple of minutes later Stacey presented him with a flimsy plastic cup which he took gratefully and sipped warily, grimacing as the bitterness nipped his taste buds.

'God, hospital coffee is even worse than the stuff we get in the nick,' he said. 'Thanks, though. At least it's hot and wet.'

The policeman obviously had no idea who she was and Stacey decided to see if she could winkle any information out of him.

'You've been here ages,' she said. 'Are you guarding someone dangerous – Wales' Most Wanted?'

'No, one of ours, injured last night.'

'How awful, what happened?'

'Sorry, but I can't really talk about it.' He drank more coffee.

'Is he very ill?'

'The doctors say he's in a medically induced coma.'

'Poor chap. I hope he makes it.'

'Me too. He's a good mate of mine. Thanks again for the coffee.'

Stacey nodded and retreated to the waiting room, knowing she'd get nothing more out of him. She wondered how Andrew was getting on at the hall, so tossed her empty cup in a nearby bin and headed towards the main entrance to find a quiet space where she could make a call. Andrew's phone rang once before it was answered.

'What's happening? Anything?' she asked.

'Coppers all over the place, never seen so many in one place since I left England.'

'What are they doing?'

'Moving stuff out of the hall, loading it into a van and keeping everyone away. Lots of boxes – no idea what they contain – and what looks to be scientific equipment, gas cylinders on trolleys, largish lumps of machinery, computer gear, that sort of stuff. I'm getting some great pictures. No other reporters about either that I can see.'

'Where exactly are you?'

'In the cafe opposite, just about to eat a proper Welsh breakfast. I haven't been spotted. How about you?'

'At the hospital in Cardiff. Mark's in intensive care, they've put a guard on his door and he's in a coma. I think I'm wasting my time. Stay put, I'll drive over and we'll work out where to go from here.'

* * *

Julie was busy sifting through piles of magazines and junk mail that littered the coffee table in Mark's flat, when she noticed the corner of a shallow cardboard box sticking out from beneath the sofa. Snagging the container with her gloved fingers, she pulled it into the light and flipped open the lid. Inside was a bundle of wadding, a sheet of paper and a photograph. She turned the picture over and was shocked to see it showed Mark in a compromising position with a young girl. Julie unfolded the paper and read the note.

'Sir, you'd better come and look at this,' she called.

Ben emerged from the kitchen, took the note from her and frowned as he read. He dropped on the sofa and examined the photo, wincing when he realised what it showed.

'This is terrible,' he muttered. 'However did Jefferies get involved with this? Who's the girl, Julie, any idea?'

She shook her head as Jack emerged from the bedroom, a thin stack of paper in his hands.

'Bank statements, boss,' he said. 'Seems Mark was saving for a rainy day or something, got over a hundred and forty grand tucked away, so why does he stay in a dump like this? You had any luck?'

Ben passed him the note and photograph. Jack skimmed and glowered.

'Where did he get all that money?' Ben asked. 'You'd think blackmailers would extort money, not pay it.'

'I reckon the cash is a sweetener,' Jack said. 'He's being blackmailed into providing this nasty lot with inside information, and by paying him they ensnare him completely. The further in he got, the more impossible it was to get away from them. The girl in the photo looks like jailbait to me. I'm guessing, but maybe one of the Consortium found out about the affair, took this photo, used it to beat Jefferies over the head with and he wasn't strong enough to resist. Bloody awful mess, boss.'

Julie pulled the wadding out of the box. Discovering traces of oil on the material she sniffed. 'Gun oil. This was the box the colonel used to send the gun.'

'OK,' Ben said. 'Let's round all this stuff up, take Mark's laptop too – you can work on that, Ian – and we'll have a search team go through the rest of the place. We should get back to the nick and interview Hammond. If she really is one of them, we must get her to talk.'

* * *

Stacey carried two mugs of tea to the table, sat by Andrew's side and stared through the window of the cafe. The van had been driven away and so had most of the police cars, leaving a couple parked at the kerb, their occupants milling around on the pavement. Nothing had moved in or out of the place for the last half hour. Stacey had been trying to contact Ben, but each time she called, his phone went to voicemail and she didn't leave a message. She had been able to talk with Sam Jenkins to let him know what she was up to and was sure she heard him salivating over the phone as he anticipated an exclusive story.

'What do we do now?' Andrew asked.

'I don't think we need to hide away any longer, looks like they've finished emptying the place. Go and find out if you can get any of them to talk and I'll knock on a few doors, ask the locals what they know – if anything. Be good to get some quotes to go with the piece. Let's give it an hour and if we can't squeeze anything out of anyone, we'll go back to the hospital in case there's any change.'

'Meet you back at my car,' Andrew said. 'I'll drive, we can pick yours up on the way back.'

The first door Stacey knocked on was opened by a diminutive, elderly woman who craned her neck to squint up at Stacey's face, owlish glasses perched on a snub nose.

'Can I help you?' she asked.

'I'm Stacey Logan, a reporter for *The Mid Wales Times*. I wonder if you can tell me anything about what happened here last night.'

'There's an awful business now, that young policeman getting shot,' the woman said. 'I saw him carried to the ambulance, poor boy. Why don't you come in for some tea and I'll tell you all about it?'

'That would be lovely, thank you, Mrs…?'

'Hughes, Ena Hughes. Come on in, *cariad*, I'll put the kettle on.'

Stacey followed the woman along the hall to the kitchen and sat at the table while her host rummaged around for cups and teaspoons.

'Awake half of the night I was,' Ena grumbled, pouring boiling water into a teapot. 'I'd been up to spend a penny and – like I always do – looked out of the window at the street. Habit of mine, never know what I'm looking for, never anything to see, but I always look, check the road.'

'And what did you see Mrs Hughes?'

'Oh, *duw duw!* Sometime after midnight, three people ran out across the road and down by the side of the hall. It was very dark, but I stayed watching, something didn't feel right. I wondered if it was kids, breaking into the hall again, little buggers. Anyway, I was about to go back to bed when I heard a bang from inside the hall.' She sipped her tea. 'I'm a farmer's daughter, Miss Logan, I know what a gun sounds like and that's what it sounded like, a gunshot. I was about to ring the police, when they arrived, cars full of them. They broke down the hall door, then an ambulance arrived. I saw them carry out a stretcher, load it in the back and the ambulance drove away fast, lights flashing.'

'How did you know it was a policeman who was shot?' Stacey asked.

'Makes sense. You don't get that many police turning out if it's one of us. Not as many or as fast. A neighbour of mine had to wait over an hour before an ambulance came for him earlier in the year, and he was having a heart attack! This lot were here in minutes last night.'

Stacey chuckled, there was nothing wrong with the old lady's thought processes.

'Have you seen anything going on at the hall over the last month or so?' she asked.

'Few people coming and going. A couple of young lads were here for about a week, dressed in overalls, might have been maintenance men. Then a few days ago, a tall, scruffy looking chap turned up and he was met by a young man in a suit. They both went inside, but only the young man came back out.'

'You don't miss much, do you?'

'Used to be part of neighbourhood watch a few years ago, when I could still get about. I guess the habit dies hard. Either that or I've become a nosey old bag with nothing better to do with her time.' She laughed. 'More tea?'

'No, thank you, Mrs Hughes, I'd better be going. If you think of anything else though, please give me a ring.' Stacey handed her a business card and stood to leave.

'I'm ninety-three,' Mrs Hughes said, 'in case you need to know for the paper, and it's Ena not Edna.'

Stacey was still giggling when she met Andrew by his car and they set off in the direction of the hospital.

Chapter thirty-one

DI James and his sergeant were making their way towards the interview rooms when Todd Morgan stuck his head out of a doorway.

'I don't suppose you gentleman have a couple of minutes to look at something, do you?'

'We're just on our way to interview Gwen Hammond, is it important?' Ben asked.

'I think you'll want to see what I've uncovered before you talk to her, might give you a bit more leverage.'

Ben nodded. 'OK, Todd. Jack, delay things for me, then come back here.'

Todd stood aside as Ben walked into the room and sat at the end of a long table, almost vanishing behind a wall of electronic equipment.

'How did you end up in here?' Ben asked. 'I thought you were happy in the custody suite.'

'That was for security more than anything and I keep telling you, hackers do like to see daylight now and again. Anyway, Sergeant Jones kicked me out, said he needed the space.'

Todd sat in front of the keyboard and with a few keystrokes the screens lit up. Jack hurried into the room and pulled up a chair.

Todd noticed his face. 'Blimey, Jack, that's one hell of a shiner, looks like you took on the Welsh rugby team in the pub – and lost.'

'I'm beginning to feel as though I have,' Jack grumbled. 'Everything's stiffening up and even coffee is too hot, makes my lip sting something horrid. What have you got then?'

'Everything you see here is connected to Gwen Hammond, daft thing is, if I'd been a bit more on the ball, we'd have worked out who she was a long time ago.'

'How so?' Ben asked.

'Remember when I was trying to trace the IP addresses? Where the computers the Consortium used were situated?' The officers nodded in unison. 'Early on I traced one back to the local authority, the council offices in Llandrindod Wells to be precise and dismissed it as more smoke screening. Thing is, Gwen Hammond works in the planning department and that's where the computer is. I've hacked into their systems and…'

'Hang on a minute, Todd,' Ben said. 'Are you telling us you've broken into the county council's computer system?'

'Yep. Dead easy too. I wonder if government organisations will ever get their heads round the fact they are not employing the best people to set up their security, they only think they are.' He grinned. 'Anyway… moving on. I managed to take over Gwen's hardware, discovered her password and then everything was accessible. I checked the times the Consortium were in the chat room or online and was able to prove Gwen used her work computer to communicate with them. I've downloaded a copy of everything on her hard drive and I'm busy working through it.' Todd pecked at the keyboard and the screen displays changed. 'These details relate to her financial situation, bank accounts, savings accounts, premium bonds, what she spends her money on and where, that sort of thing.'

'You hacked into her bank as well?' Ben was astounded.

'I hacked into everything with her name on it, everything I could get into, that is.' He smiled. 'Like Cavendish, she has a stash of Bitcoins, maximum allowance of premium bonds, ISAs, the lot. Far too much capital to be explained away, she doesn't earn anything like that sort of money. I guess when she recruited her nephew, she thought she was doing him a favour. I wonder if Cavendish knew he was being employed by his aunt?'

'Anything else? I'm not sure we can hold her on that and if we let her go I feel it in my water she'll run,' Jack grouched.

'Impatient aren't you, Sergeant? Never been told you have to wait for good things? I'm still digging around in Gwen's hard drive and tucked away somewhere in there is the encryption code to the rest of their system, then we'll know who the other two are. Maybe you should tell her we're already in, make her give up the rest of the group.'

* * *

The interview had not gone well. Gwen's solicitor – unsurprisingly Steve Bowen from Cardiff – had advised his client not to answer or comment on any of the questions the officers asked and she took heed, refusing to speak at all. After half an hour of an utterly one-sided interrogation, the officers gave up, Gwen was returned to her cell and an application made to extend the length of her custody.

Jack was not pleased with the situation at all. 'Bloody woman and that pompous arse of a solicitor! Do you reckon he has anything to do with the Consortium, boss?'

'I don't think so, as far as I can tell he's just doing his job, been at it for years defending criminals. We must dig up something good enough to keep Hammond remanded, some hard evidence would be useful instead of all this cyberspace rubbish. I can't get my head round any of it and don't think the magistrate will be able to either.'

'Maybe the search team will uncover something useful at her house,' Julie said.

'We can but hope,' Ben muttered. 'Mark's still out of it in hospital with no signs he's improving, so all we have is the word of a possibly dying man, who would appear to have been a corrupt police officer, against the word of a local councillor – if she'd bloody say anything.'

'We need a break, boss. The team's been at it for weeks now and the last few days have been ridiculous. Go and see DCI Ambrose, give him a full report, then send everyone home, including you and me. I'll have a word with Julie, but it'd be great if you and Stacey could come over. We can unwind together and start again fresh in the morning.' He smiled. 'Bring your cossies and I'll fire up the hot tub, it's just what we all need.'

* * *

The friends luxuriated in steaming water and felt their tension drifting away. It was a gentle, warm evening and a slight breeze deterred swarming midges. They had eaten well and after an awkward few weeks, were beginning to relax in each other's company again. Jack and Julie lounged against each other and held hands, while Stacey played footsie with Ben until he grabbed her leg and threatened to pull her under.

'For God's sake, will you two behave?' Jack scolded. 'It's like being with a couple of kids. I was enjoying unwinding, this water's working miracles on my aching muscles. Gotta make the most of it while we can, it's been a tough couple of days and there's more to come.'

'How much more work is there?' Stacey asked.

'Masses of it,' Ben groaned. 'We have to have another go at Gwen Hammond and find out if she can tell us who the others are, maybe even get a confession out of her.

That would help enormously. Todd's still working on her online footprint. I told him and Ian to go home, but they refused and kept at it. We've been over the letter we found at Mark's flat that the colonel sent with the gun – no fingerprints or DNA unfortunately but at least it has cleared up a good chunk of the investigation. The note clearly states Mark was involved in the deaths of Jeremy Cavendish and John Williams, and implied he made the call to Gwen from the cells the day Jeremy was arrested using the lad's phone.' He swished the warm water about with one hand. 'James Spencer confirmed Jefferies did ask to inspect Jeremy's property that morning, but he hadn't recorded the request as nothing was removed. What all this doesn't explain is why.'

'He was being blackmailed,' Jack said. 'Shagging an underage girl isn't going to do anything for your career – or the rest of your life come to that – although I have no idea what was going on in his head when he started the affair. It's possible he thought she was older. Do we know who she is yet?'

'Not a clue,' Ben said, 'but like everything else, we're working on it.'

'Ben told me you have another front-page story tomorrow,' Julie said, smiling at her friend.

Stacey nodded.

'You still haven't told me how you found out what was going on in Ammanford,' Ben grumbled.

'One of my informants tipped me off and it goes without saying that every journalist has to protect her sources,' Stacey said, 'so there's no point in asking me anything about it, cos I'm not going to tell you. Poor old Mark though. I like Mark and hope he gets better.'

'Probably better for him if he didn't,' Jack muttered ominously.

The group lapsed into silence. A few minutes later, Julie hauled herself out of the steaming water and padded towards the house. She returned with a bottle of champagne, ice cold, condensation dripping from the glass. She handed it to her partner before slipping gratefully into the warm water.

'Isn't bubbly a bit premature?' Jack asked. 'We haven't solved the case yet, heaps of rubbish to wade through before we can celebrate.'

Julie smiled at him. 'This is for something else.'

'What else?' he asked. 'Me avoiding being shot and able to annoy the rest of you for a while longer?'

'Yeah that… and something special.' Julie caught Stacey's eye, and sent a silent warning to her friend to look surprised. 'Jack, I'm pregnant.'

Jack stared at her, mouth wide open, for once utterly speechless.

Julie laughed and splashed him with water. 'Well, say something can't you?'

'I don't know what to say, I really don't. A baby? My baby? Well, yours too, of course, but me – a dad? Bloody hell, how long have you known?'

'A while now. I'm three months gone. The baby should be born around the middle of February, next year. Are you pleased, *cariad*?'

'Pleased? I'm delighted! Wow, me a dad. That'll take some getting used to. Here, Ben, get the champers open, will you? I want to give my woman a hug, isn't she marvellous?'

Ben worked on the cork and eased it out of the bottle with a satisfying pop.

'Here's to you both, well, all three of you. Congratulations!' Ben swigged directly from the bottle before passing it to Stacey who toasted the happy couple. Jack took the champagne from her and drank deeply.

'What an unbelievable day this has been,' he sighed, stroked Julie's hair and planted tiny kisses on her ear. 'I'm totally exhausted and totally and completely happy. Have you told your Mam and Da? They'll be overjoyed. We'd better start thinking about names.'

Julie giggled. 'Bit too soon for that, but we've plenty of time to come up with a good Welsh name.' She pulled herself out of the tub and slipped into a towelling robe. 'I'm off to make hot chocolate, help soak up the fizz and suggest we all have an early night, tomorrow is going to be hectic.'

* * *

That night as Julie snuggled up to her partner, she remembered hearing the gunshot at the hall and shivered. Jack pulled her closer and felt her relax.

'You are pleased about the baby aren't you, *cariad*?' she asked.

'Of course. I always wanted to be a dad, even when I was young, but could never see quite how fatherhood could happen when I couldn't find a woman who'd put up with me for longer than a few weeks – until I met you, that is. A baby is such wonderful news and February isn't far away. I'll have to get started on the spare room now, must have somewhere decent for the little chap when he arrives.'

'Or chapess, when she arrives. It could be a girl.'

'I don't care, really I don't, the whole idea is amazing.'

'Oh, Jack.' Julie began to cry quietly. 'What would have happened if you'd been the one who was shot, if it was you who was in intensive care?'

'Sush, Jules, don't. It wasn't, I'm here and I'm safe.'

'Just remember, DS Trent, you promised me you'd *never* do anything like this again without discussing it with me first and I mean to hold you to that promise. If you're going to be a father, you'll have to be more responsible.'

Jack chuckled. 'Responsible sounds boring if you ask me. Now, snuggle down, we can't stay awake all night chatting, lots to do in the morning. I've been awake since the wee small hours of the morning, and hurled myself down a flight of stairs.' He kissed her and wrapped his long body round hers. 'Oh, and this good Welsh name you have in mind? Just make sure I can say it,' he mumbled.

The Mid Wales Times – 22nd August
POLICE OFFICER SHOT IN AMMANFORD by Stacey Logan

Detective Constable Mark Jefferies was shot in the early hours of 21st August during an operation on the outskirts of Lower Brynamman. Acting on information received, the abandoned working men's club was raided by a large team of officers from Dyfed Powys Police. The raid is believed to be connected to a similar operation earlier in the year when a clandestine laboratory was dismantled and a large quantity of deadly ecstasy pills seized. It is understood DC Jefferies was a member of a team working on the ongoing investigation. He is in a serious condition in the Intensive Care Unit at Cardiff Hospital. Doctors have confirmed his injuries are life threatening and he is being kept sedated in a medically induced coma.
No one from the police was available for comment, but we understand an arrest has been made in connection with the case.

Chapter thirty-two

Ben tapped his coffee mug with a ballpoint pen to cease the noisy chatter rolling around the conference room. DCI Ambrose had ventured out of his office and sat next to his inspector at the head of the table. A pile of paper bags littered the shiny surface, spilling out various Danish pastries and doughnuts – Jack had visited the bakers on the way in. He sat next to his partner, a self-satisfied grin twisting his bruised and battered face.

'Let's have some hush, people,' Ben said. 'DCI Ambrose would like a word.'

Ambrose cleared his throat.

'Firstly, I would like to say well done; excellent work over the last few days. I have read through the reports with great interest and passed on your results to the Chief Super. There are, however, quite a few loose ends to tie up, as I'm sure you're aware. Any progress with Gwen Hammond, Inspector?'

'No, sir. Her solicitor is still advising her not to say anything and she's doing exactly that. Haven't got a word out of her since she was arrested. Todd Morgan has put together a file containing all her financial and employment details, phone records, credit card spending and a printout listing all internet communication. We can prove she's been in contact with the other members of the Consortium and Todd is working on decoding those conversations. I think we have enough to be able to charge her with conspiracy to supply. She certainly has more money in the bank than she has ever earned – if you include the Bitcoins – we can charge her under the Proceeds of Crime Act, if nothing else. It'll give us a breathing space and if we work at it, I'm sure we'll be able to convince the magistrates she's a flight risk.'

'Are we any closer to discovering the identities of the other two?'

'Not yet, sir, but Constable Bradshaw is working on Constable Jefferies' laptop. I'm hoping the encryption code will be on his hard drive. Todd is making good progress and once we've cracked it, all should become clear.'

'We can but hope.' Ambrose glanced at Jack. 'Bloody hell, Sergeant, your face is a dreadful mess, shouldn't you take some leave?'

'No thanks, sir, I'm fine; never better. I learned last night I'm going to be a dad soon. How amazing is that?'

Ambrose raised his eyebrows in surprise. 'Congratulations – to you both,' he said, smiling at Julie. 'Nice to have some good news for once. Ben, do you need anything from me?'

'We're fine, sir, thank you. We'll charge Hammond, she'll go to court in the morning and I'll keep on at our trained hackers, see if they can speed things up. I'm hoping Hammond will be remanded with what we have at the moment, but there's no guarantee.'

DCI Ambrose nodded, got to his feet and helped himself to the last doughnut. 'Make sure you keep me updated,' he said as he left the room and headed back upstairs to his comfortable office.

* * *

Stacey arrived home feeling happier than she had in weeks. Spending the evening with her friends had been good for her and being able to share Julie's exciting news at last was wonderful. She'd called in at the local supermarket on the way home to restock her cupboards and dumped an armful of shopping bags on the table, before putting the kettle on. She had begun emptying the bags when her phone rang; she answered it in the office.

'Hey, Stace, Andrew here. How's it going?'

'Good thanks, you?'

'Same, same. Nice piece on the front page this morning, thanks for the mention.'

'You took a great photo. A line of coppers passing boxes and loading them in a van, framed perfectly by the old hall in the background, of course you should get the credit. What can I do for you?'

'I've been summoned,' Andrew said. 'Sam wants me in the office and I wondered if you'd like a lift to Brecon.'

'Wouldn't mind tagging along, actually, thanks. When do I have to be ready?'

'I'll leave home now and pick you up, but there's no rush. Our esteemed editor only said I had to attend, didn't give me a particular time. I'll see you soon.'

* * *

An hour and a half later, the reporters were sitting in Sam's untidy office. Unusually, their editor was smiling. He held up the day's edition of the paper and pointed at the front page.

'Now, this is more like it,' he enthused. 'An exclusive and a brilliant photo. You two make a good partnership. How did you hear about the raid?'

'Aw, come on, boss, you know better than to ask.' Stacey smiled at him. 'Surely, it doesn't matter how as long as we did.'

'True, true. Who have they arrested, any idea?'

'Not officially, but I understand the individual has been charged and will be in the magistrates' court in the morning. Obviously, we'll both be there too.'

'Make sure you are and keep on it. This is the biggest story the paper has got its hands on for a while. Any news on DC Jefferies?'

'Still in a coma. I checked with the hospital this morning, but they're not saying much.'

'I could go down and hang around if you like, boss,' Andrew suggested. 'Haven't got much else on at the moment.'

'How are you getting on with the fraud thing, the missing charity money?' Sam asked.

'Still working my way through, haven't forgotten, but I reckon this is a little more important, don't you?'

Sam nodded thoughtfully.

'You asked me to come in to see you, boss,' Andrew said. 'Was it just to say well done or did you need me for something else?' Andrew asked.

'Oh, yes, so I did, wanted to ask if you'd like a permanent position. I can't see the point of keeping you on probation, you're proving to be useful, so how about it?'

'Great! I mean thanks. Yes, I'd like that very much.'

'Even when you're back covering local fundraising and rugby matches? It isn't always as exciting as this, you know.'

'Yep, even writing that stuff. If things are too quiet I can always work on my novel.'

'What novel?' Sam asked.

'He's winding you up, Sam,' Stacey said. 'He hasn't started one yet, as far as I know. Whippersnapper sees himself as an author, but I think that's a way off yet.'

* * *

Stacey was in her office sorting through the clutch of photographs which had built up on her laptop, when Ben walked through the back door of the cottage and kissed her on the back of her neck. She wrapped an arm around his neck and pulled his face closer so she could kiss him properly.

'Hi, Sherlock, you're good and early.'

'Good to be here. I've seen enough of the station for the day. It's been another hard one. Have you had a good one?'

'Not bad thanks. Went to Brecon to see Sam. I don't think I've ever seen him as happy. He does love an exclusive.'

'I saw the article. You never cease to amaze me, have an uncanny knack of being in the right place at the right time.'

'Good trick to have if you're a reporter.' Stacey laughed. 'I'll just finish off here and make a start on supper. Help yourself to a drink.'

Ben peered over her shoulder at the screen. 'That's a picture of the garden party, isn't it? I thought you'd left your cameras at home.'

'Yes I did, but I used my camera phone, sorry. I'm trying to sort out my picture library, far too much in it, so I'm weeding out the bad ones. Here, look at this enchanting shot of the grounds covered with little tents.' Stacey tapped the keyboard and photos scrolled slowly by.

'Hang on, Pumpkin, back up a minute, would you?'

Ben examined one shot closely, frowning with concentration.

'Can you enlarge this or anything?' he asked. 'I want a better look at this group here, standing by the yellow tent.'

Stacey worked the keyboard and by cropping the photo, she enlarged the mid-section.

'That's Robert Evans,' she said, pointing out a figure standing next to the canvas. 'Izzy's father.'

Ben stabbed at the screen with his finger. 'And that's Gwen Hammond! What was she doing there? That's the woman we've got in custody, a county councillor who sits on the planning committee, ideal position to track down suitable properties for labs.'

'Come on, Ben, you don't think Robert has anything to do with this, do you? He lost his daughter to these poisonous pills, has set up a support group and a trust with his wife to try and stop others losing their kids. He can't possibly be involved, that would be too weird.'

'Just about as weird as Jeremy Cavendish's auntie recruiting her nephew – he's dead too, remember.'

'Talk about keeping it in the family. Do you think Jeremy knew she was involved?'

Ben shook his head. 'I can't see we'll ever know unless she decides to come clean. Can you print off a couple of these pictures for me?'

'No problem.' Stacey carried the laptop through to the office and Ben followed.

'Can I use your phone?' he asked.

'Of course, help yourself while I get the printer working.'

Ben picked up the receiver and dialled, waiting impatiently for someone to answer. The voicemail clicked on.

'Hello. This is Todd, you know what to do after the tone.'

'Todd, DI James. Can you give me a call when you get this message? It's fairly urgent.' He banged the phone down. 'Bugger, I wonder where he is?'

'Give him a break, Sherlock, he gets to have time off too, doesn't he? He's not even a copper, so you can't order him about like you do the others. Here.' She held out a photo. 'Will that do?'

'Perfect. Can you send a copy to Todd via email? I want him to look at it as soon as possible.'

'No problem, give me his address and go and get the kettle on. I can't work with you hovering.'

Ben wandered into the kitchen, filled the kettle and was just about to switch it on when his mobile rang.

'DI James.'

'Todd here. What can I do for you? I'm in the middle of supper.'

'Sorry to bother you, but my partner is sending you a photo of Gwen Hammond and a guy called Robert Evans, he's the father of the young girl who died in June. Any chance you could trawl the net, see if you can discover anything about him?'

'Of course, what are you looking for?'

'I want to know if there's a connection between Gwen and Robert. They look chummy in the picture, but may have just met that evening. If you have a word with Ian, he'll be able to provide you the details of Evans' address, phone numbers, that sort of thing. Any chance you can take a look this evening?'

Todd chuckled. 'I'm glad I don't actually work for you,' he said. 'You're a hard taskmaster. I've only just finished for the day and here you are trying to get me at it again.'

'It's important, Todd. I wouldn't ask if it wasn't.'

'I'm winding you up, Inspector. Ian's here with me, so we'll get on with it now.'

'Are you still both at the station?'

'No, we're at home. Hang on a mo.' The line went quiet before Todd came back on. 'The photo has arrived, I'll see what I can do with it and contact you if I find anything. OK if I use your partner's email address?'

'Yeah, that's fine, she won't mind. Any idea how long you'll need?'

'Not a clue, depends what I find. I'll be in touch.' Todd broke the connection as Stacey walked into the kitchen and started preparing supper. Ben rummaged about in the larder and emerged with a bottle of red wine, pulled the cork, poured two glasses and handed one to his partner.

'What do you know about the Evanses?' he asked.

'Not much, only met them because of what happened to Izzy. I interviewed them after she died, usual sort of stuff about wanting to help others. Robert said they were going to set up a trust – The Izzy Evans Trust. He'd been saving in a fund for Izzy's education and as she wasn't going to need it, he was prepared to donate the money. They seemed like a normal couple, struggling with their grief. He's a gem dealer, just back from Thailand, but has travelled all over the world. I guess you'd describe his wife, Mair, as a yummy mummy, a lady who lunches. I don't think she works, although she's flung herself into the trust as a way of keeping busy, it would seem.'

'I wonder what the link is between them and Gwen Hammond?' Ben mused as his partner put a shepherd's pie in the Aga and shut the door.

Chapter thirty-three

After hanging up his jacket, collecting a coffee from the machine and checking in with his team, Ben went in search of Todd and Ian. He found them in the meeting room, working side by side behind the dense barrier of electronic equipment.

'Morning, boys, anything for me?'

'Morning, sir, yeah, we think so,' Ian said. 'Pull up a seat.' Ian moved his chair closer to his companion so Ben could fit behind the desk.

'Todd's been at it since you rang last night and he can prove a link between Hammond and Evans: they were both recorded in the Consortium's chat room. He's also found another stash of Bitcoins – on Evans' hard drive. The best news of all is we can finally access their conversations and the pair of them are in it up to their necks!' Ian sounded triumphant, a wide grin splitting his face.

'That's brilliant!' Ben said. 'Show me.'

Todd worked on one of the keyboards and a transcript of a conversation which took place in May was displayed. The more Ben read, the more delighted he grew.

'Todd, this is wonderful stuff! How did you manage to access Evans' computer?'

Todd tapped his nose. 'Trick of the trade,' he said. 'You can't ask me questions like that because you're not going to like the answers, and hackers don't give up their secrets. I'm sure I've found enough to put Evans firmly in the centre of things, he's the cashier you've been searching for. The money man. I've been able to prove he buys the supplies – chemicals, equipment, that sort of stuff. It also appears he arranges the sale of the finished product and definitely launders the money before it's distributed within the group.'

The door at the end of the room swung open and Jack Trent walked in.

'Jack, come and see this,' Ben said. 'These two have found our cashier. Robert Evans, Izzy's dad.'

'You're joking, surely. Izzy's father involved with making the rubbish which killed his daughter? No way!'

'It's true and we can prove it; well, these guys can.'

'So, who's the colonel?' Jack asked.

'That's about the only thing we can't tell you,' Ian said. 'He or she has covered their tracks so bloody well, we keep hitting walls; it's like being stuck in the middle of a maze which doesn't have a way out. We'll keep working on it though, we might get lucky. Todd has printed out all this stuff, there's a folder on the table containing the main points. It's absolutely conclusive though, no way will Evans be able to wriggle out of it.' Ian grinned. 'By the time you arrest him and get back here, the rest will be ready for you.'

'One more down and another one to go then?' Jack muttered. 'Bloody computers, they make all sorts of nasty things far too bloody easy.'

'I never had you down for a Luddite, Sergeant.' Todd laughed. 'This lot may have used the internet to get rich, but we've just used to it catch them – "beyond all reasonable doubt". You'll have two good convictions out of this. Patience and a bit more work might bring you a third.'

'As long as the jury can get their heads round the evidence, I'm not entirely sure I can.'

'You're only suspicious of the net because you don't understand it like I do. I'll give you lessons if you're interested.'

Jack humphed. 'Let's go, boss. We'll bring Evans here and find out what he's got to say for himself, although what that can possibly be, I have no idea.'

* * *

Ben and Jack marched straight into Mr Evans' office at the Brecon Business Park and ignored the protests of his secretary who trotted in behind them.

'I'm sorry, Robert,' she said. 'I asked them to wait, but they took no notice.'

'It's fine, Jenni. Can I get you something to drink, gentlemen?'

'No, thank you, sir. We've come to escort you to the station. We are arresting you on suspicion of conspiracy to supply class A drugs.'

Jack recited the rest of the caution as all colour left Evans' face to be replaced by a damp shininess. He didn't say a word as he was led downstairs, posted in the back of the car and driven to Builth police station. He was processed quickly and a little over an hour later, was sitting in an interview room staring across a metal table at the officers.

The prisoner had refused access to a solicitor, and also declined to take up the offer of a phone call. He appeared to have shrunk during his trip to the station and his brief confinement in a cell. His belt and tie had been confiscated and his open collar was stained with sweat, shirt sticking to his chest. His eyes flicked warily, trying not to catch the glare of either man sitting opposite him, and he continually rubbed his hands together as though washing them.

Ben opened the folder in front of him. Todd had been as good as his word and pages of conversations had been transcribed. He picked one at random and began to read out loud.

'We've lost not only the product, but the equipment too. Have you any idea how much all that stuff costs? We've got to replace the lot…'

'Stop!' Robert said and held up his hands. 'Just stop. I know what I said.'

'You don't deny this conversation?' Ben asked.

'No. I don't deny any of it. That was me. I am the cashier and I was part of the Consortium. How did you work it out? Did the colonel send you?'

'No, why would he?'

'When you arrived at the office this morning, I thought…'

'What did you think?' Jack growled.

The prisoner groaned and covered his face with his hands, massaging the skin.

'It doesn't matter, won't matter what I think for a long time if you have your way. Am I right, gentlemen?'

'Why? That's what I want to know,' Jack demanded. 'Why on earth did you get involved? I guess greed played a part at the beginning, but how could you carry on making ecstasy when those pills killed your own daughter? Even a hard-hearted bastard might think twice, don't you think? Or is money the most important thing in your life?' DS Trent leant over the table, almost spitting in the man's face.

'I didn't have a choice,' Evans mumbled. 'I wanted to stop, but the colonel wouldn't let me go. He controlled all of us utterly. A truly evil man, not a speck of compassion in him.'

'How did he control you?'

'He knew about the skeletons we each had in our cupboards, our nasty little secrets. I thought it was only me he had something on, but when I met Gwen at the garden party earlier in the year, it turned out he had something on her as well.'

'What?' Jack spat at the man. 'What did he have on you?'

Evans sighed again and hid behind his hands.

'I brought some stuff into the UK, from Thailand, when I was on a buying trip.'

'What sort of stuff? Do you mean drugs?'

'Yeah. Cannabis resin. Ten Kilos. I'd hidden it in a consignment of cheap amber – amber's classed as "resin" on customs documentation – and I've imported so much over the years, no one looked at it twice. Somehow – and I don't know how – the colonel found out and threatened to ruin me. I really tried to get out after Izzy died, but couldn't. I set up the trust to try to absolve myself and it helped Mair deal with her loss. I felt so… guilty.'

'That's because you are!' Jack hissed nastily. 'Those awful pills you and your gang were churning out were killing people, you knew it and did nothing. Who is this bloke, the colonel? Tell us where we can find him.'

'I can't,' Evans wailed. 'I don't know who he is. Never met him. He spoke in the chat rooms using a device to disguise his voice and I have no idea who he is. I asked Gwen – Miss Hammond – about it when we met at the party, but she didn't know either.' He sighed heavily. 'He was able to keep her under control because he discovered she'd helped herself to some local charity fund. It wasn't a lot of money, a few thousand; I don't know why she bothered, but somehow this guy found out and she was trapped.' He paused. 'Can I have a drink?'

Jack nodded, went to the door, shouted down the corridor and waited for one of the custody officers to fetch some water.

Ben rubbed his temples and regarded the man opposite him. He knew his prisoner was telling the truth, they wouldn't be able to catch the colonel using this broken man. Ben almost felt sorry for Evans until he remembered how many people had died as a consequence of his actions. Mark Jefferies was still in Cardiff hospital's high dependency unit neither alive nor dead, and three young people had been fatally poisoned.

Jack placed a bottle of water on the table. Evans drank greedily and wiped his lips on a shirt cuff.

'I think we'll take a break, Sergeant.' Ben hauled himself up from the chair and stood over his prisoner. 'Are you sure you don't want a solicitor? You understand we intend to charge you for conspiracy to murder among other things?'

Evans nodded. 'I'm glad to get it off my chest. I've been living this bloody awful lie for so long now, I'm exhausted by it all. Will you ring Mair for me? Tell her where I am?'

'You could do that yourself – if you want to.'

'No. I can't bear to talk to her after what I've done and I know she won't want to talk to me – probably never again – so if you'd let her know about this mess, I'd be grateful.'

After Robert Evans had been charged and locked in a cell, Ben called the rest of the team to the meeting room where Todd and Ian still hammered away at keyboards, muttering to each other in hacker-chat as they pruned proof of misdeeds from cyberspace.

'How did the interview go, sir?' James Spencer asked, unable to mask his excitement.

'Good. It went well. Robert Evans is confessing.'

'Result!' Spencer pounded Julie on the back until he spotted Jack glowering at him.

'Settle down, gang.' Ben grinned at them. 'We still don't know the identity of the colonel. Evans says he'd never met the individual, but confirmed he was being blackmailed. So was Gwen Hammond apparently, something about pinching money from a local charity, but as she's still refusing to talk to us, we can't confirm that.'

‘Maybe she’ll be a little more co-operative now her partner in crime is sharing. Gotta be worth a go, boss,’ Jack said.

‘Next on the to-do list. I wonder what else the nice Miss Hammond has been up to. Dodgy dealings in the planning department is surely a given, access to privileged information, and if you’re an elected councillor that’s serious enough, without any of the other stuff.’ Ben looked at his team and smiled. ‘I’m proud of you, all of you. You’ve worked hard on this investigation and although we cocked things up at the start, we’ve made up for it, so well done.’

He turned to the men working at the computer. ‘Todd and Ian, you’ve done enough for today. I was told you were in at four this morning, so you’ve already done a full day’s work. Get off now and start again in the morning. The rest of you, make sure your reports are up to date and you can knock off too. I’ll nip upstairs and have a word with DCI Ambrose, then I’m done for the day. We’re nearly there, folks, just the colonel to go and I’m sure we’ll find him. Bloody well done!’

Chapter thirty-four

The Mid Wales Times – 25th August
DRUGS AND MURDER CONSPIRACY PLOT: TWO CHARGED by Stacey Logan

Two people appeared in court yesterday charged with conspiracy to supply class A drugs, and murder. Gwen Hammond, 52, of Builth Wells, a councillor on the county council's planning committee, and Mr Robert Evans, 48, a gemstone dealer and father of Izzy Evans, whose body was discovered at the rave close to the village of Garth in June of this year, are both facing prosecution.

The case has been linked to raids earlier this year at two properties in the local area when drugs and equipment were seized by police. A serving officer, DC Mark Jefferies, remains in hospital and is being maintained in a medically induced coma, his condition has not improved.

The case has been passed to Crown Court and will be heard later in the year. Both Hammond and Evans only spoke to confirm their names and addresses and have been remanded in custody as they were considered a flight risk.

Mair Evans, mother of Izzy, attended court supported by a friend, but made no comment.

The case is ongoing and further arrests are expected.

* * *

The large kitchen table in Stacey's cottage was surrounded, chairs jammed in so everyone could sit together. Todd and Ian had arrived bearing bottles of wine, Jack and Julie sat closely together talking quietly, while Ben and Stacey – with the assistance of Andrew Carr – dished out food. They were just about to tuck in to a rich beef casserole and dumplings, when there was a knock at the door. Ben went to answer it and came back to the kitchen with James Spencer, still wearing his uniform.

Stacey looked up from the table and smiled. 'Glad you could make it. I was beginning to wonder if you would.'

'Sgt Jones has kept me at it all day,' he said, 'but I wasn't going to miss this evening. Thanks for the invite. I'm glad you gave me directions, I'd never have found you otherwise.'

'Well, you're here now and officially off duty. Pour him some wine, Ian, and shove up a touch so he can squeeze in.'

Stacey placed a loaded plate in front of the latecomer and he tucked in as though he hadn't eaten in a week. An hour later, the casserole pot was empty and the group moved into the garden to sprawl on the lawn in the evening sunshine.

'This is pleasant,' Ben said, 'everyone together. Thanks for arranging supper, Pumpkin. Don't worry about the clearing up, we'll see to that, you did the cooking. Raise your glasses everyone in a toast to the chef, a lovely meal.'

'My pleasure. Glad you're all here,' she hesitated, 'well – nearly everyone. I'm not sure you can all stay the night though, unless anyone wants to sleep on the lawn.'

Jack chuckled and lay down, resting his head on Julie's lap.

'That'll do for me,' he said, 'as long as my pillow doesn't object and the dew's not too heavy. I might shrink.'

'No chance of that, *cariad*' – Julie giggled – 'if anything, you're growing, I reckon you need to go on a diet.' She poked a finger in his midriff and tickled until he caught hold of her wrist and kissed the back of her hand.

'It's not my fault. You shouldn't feed me so well.'

Stacey heard her phone ringing inside the cottage and leapt up to answer it, only to discover it wasn't her phone, but Ben's. She carried the mobile out to the garden and handed it to her partner.

'DI James,' he said and listened, the smile quickly vanishing from his face.

'I see, yes.' He listened some more. 'Thank you for informing me, sir, yes I'll let the others know.' Another pause. 'Yes, I will, sir, and I hope you have a good weekend.'

Ben ended the call.

'That was Charlie Ambrose. Mark's dead. His mother asked for the machines to be turned off as he hadn't shown any signs of improvement.'

'How awful!' Stacey said.

'At least he won't have to face the music for his involvement in this awful business,' Jack muttered. 'If he'd survived, he'd have been sent down for sure. Ex-coppers don't get an easy ride inside and one who had been sleeping with an underage girl would have been so much dead meat within days.'

'But it's so bloody sad,' Stacey said. 'I really liked Mark and everyone makes mistakes.'

'They do, that's true, but this was a complete lack of judgement,' Jack said. 'He was a corrupt copper, tempted by the dark side. How much of the story will come out, boss?'

'Hopefully, none of it. DCI Ambrose wants to keep it quiet and leave things as they are, a dedicated officer shot in the line of duty. Hammond and Evans have no idea who the conspirator was, so it's not likely to come out… as long as we can keep the press quiet that is.' Ben glanced at the two reporters.

Andrew protested. 'You can't do that! That's outrageous! Cover up a thing like this? Why would you do that?'

'We have to retain the trust the local community has in the force and something like this could put us back years.'

'Even so, I can't see you'll get away with it, even if you manage to silence me and Stacey. What happens when you catch the colonel? He knows who the Consortium were and all their secrets, so he'll spill the beans, surely?'

'We haven't caught him yet, though, have we?'

'But you will… won't you?' Andrew's face was flushed with anger. 'You're still looking for him and when you pull him in and put him in the dock, he'll say anything to save his skin. There's no way you can keep this quiet.'

'I don't think we'll ever trace him,' Todd mumbled. 'He's covered his tracks beautifully and seems to have vanished in the system. I've been working on it for weeks and still no closer to working out who he is or where he's based. Ian and I have been reading through the decoded conversations and he's good, this guy. He was definitely the brains behind the scheme and he's in the wind. Nothing he said in any of the chat rooms provides any clue to his identity at all. Look how he managed to arrange the collection of the pills from the first lab. He obviously has contacts, I wouldn't be surprised if he actually is a Colonel in the army, but there's not a chance I'm hacking the British Forces systems. That way leads to a cell, without passing anything that looks like go.'

'Not good enough!' Andrew spluttered. 'You can't sweep all this under the carpet, three kids died and it was only luck that allowed Jack to walk away.'

'Skill, not luck, whippersnapper,' Jack growled. 'What do you think you'd achieve if you wrote about this? Jefferies had been a good copper for years and if the story gets out it'll probably finish his mother off. Don't you think he's been punished enough, he is dead after all?'

Andrew struggled to his feet and stomped off towards the end of the garden, Stacey followed him.

'Hey, come on, Jack's right you know,' she said. 'We got a great story out of this, sometimes you don't need to tell it all.'

'This isn't right. I can't see any of the national papers allowing themselves to be brow beaten like this. Whatever happened to publish and be damned?'

'We're not working for a national, though, are we? Just a small local paper with a devoted readership. I can't see anyone is going to want to read about a well-known and well-respected local copper who was caught by a devious individual who blackmailed him into something as bad as this. Perhaps the force will change their view of things if they do manage to discover who and where the colonel is, but you heard Todd, that isn't likely. Everyone has to make compromises sometimes and this is one of those times. We're lucky, you and I, to have the contacts within the force we have. There will be other stories and by everyone staying on speaking terms, it makes our jobs easier.'

Andrew didn't look convinced and stared at the vastness of the Epynt ranges, watching the sun as it began to sink behind the ridge.

Stacey looped her arm in his and squeezed. 'Maybe you can use the details for a plot in the novel you're threatening to write? Nothing is ever wasted. Come back to the party before all the wine is gone.'

The Mid Wales Times – 6th November

MAXIMUM SENTENCES FOR THE CONSORTIUM by Stacey Logan and Andrew Carr

Long jail sentences were handed down yesterday at Cardiff Crown Court to Gwen Hammond and Robert Evans, both of Builth Wells, Powys.

They were convicted of conspiracy to manufacture and supply illegal substances, and three counts of manslaughter. Hammond was also found guilty of malpractice in a public office and fraud. It was revealed she had used her position on the County Council's planning committee to procure properties subsequently used as "cook houses" to produce ecstasy. It was proved the deaths earlier in the year were caused as a direct result of ingesting the drug. Evans' own daughter was the first victim, yet he continued to assist a group – known as the Consortium – to produce the deadly pills.

Mair Evans made a statement outside the court that she would never forgive her husband for what he had done and as far as she was concerned, he could rot in prison. "I hope he's never released," she said, "that he dies in jail. I never want to have anything to do with him ever again. He has taken away everything I ever cared about and deserves to be punished."

Summing up, Mr Justice Thomas said, "You have both demonstrated an utter lack of compassion towards your victims, and greed appeared to be your only motive for these dreadful crimes. I have no hesitation in sentencing you both to the maximum penalty under the law. You are both sentenced to life in prison and must serve at least twenty years before either of you can be considered for release."

Gwen Hammond's solicitor read a prepared statement to waiting press informing them it was his client's intention to appeal against the harsh sentence imposed. No comment was offered by Evans' legal team.

Epilogue

Standing on a balcony overlooking the early morning city, the colonel sipped strong, black coffee and peered through yellow smog. A sandstorm had blown in overnight and the air still held on to thousands of specks of desert sand. On the streets below, local shopkeepers were sweeping away piles of the stuff and school children picked their way past the mounds as they chattered on their way to school. Close by, the call to prayer drifted through the morning, echoing between the buildings on the island of Zamalek, floating in the middle of the Nile. He could hear at least three different Imams summoning their congregations and the voices mingled pleasantly.

He had always loved Cairo, the bustle, the swarming hordes, the sounds and smells of the place, and had planned to retire here. Things changed a little after the Arab Spring, but he was well known in the district, been visiting for years and had purchased his flat, during the presidency of Mubarak, in a formally grand building opposite several foreign embassies. The sun was already hot and he planned a trip to the nearby fish gardens, a relaxing place to spend his day beneath the palms. He had arranged to meet up with his technical advisor, his IT specialist. The young man had proved invaluable during the last moneymaking scheme and the colonel was anxious to stay in touch. The man might be useful in the future.

When the Consortium began to fall, one after the other, the colonel wondered whether the police would be able to track him, even though his contact had assured him he was untouchable. He smiled – free and clear, that was obvious. He'd monitored news websites in the UK and read about the court proceedings with interest. That brainless man, Evans, had been only too eager to unburden himself and once he folded, Hammond quickly followed. He was still flabbergasted Hammond had involved her nephew in the scheme – he hadn't predicted that – and was sure in his own mind this was where the scheme had begun to unravel. How anyone could have been so stupid, he failed to comprehend. Next time he set up a scheme, he would be more careful with his choice of staff.

He went in out of the sun and poured another cup of thick Turkish coffee to accompany his breakfast of sweet bread rolls and hard-boiled eggs. No, the investigation had ended favourably, but he felt incomplete somehow, needed something to occupy him during his – hopefully – long and happy retirement. His mind wandered back to the mountains of Mid Wales and the Sennybridge camp where he'd trained as a young soldier many years ago and remembered the collector and the part he had played. That man may be useful again, and after all… the colonel now had something on him, another dirty little secret to be used as leverage in the future.

He switched on his laptop and waited while the connection sorted itself out. He noticed he had an email which had filtered its way through the convoluted mesh of systems his IT man had set up for him. Clicking to open the correspondence he felt the smile slip from his face as he read the message.

To: Thecolonel@yahoo.com
From: Toddthehacker@gmail.com
Subject: A warning!

I don't know who you are or where you are, not yet, but I will. Wherever you pop up on the net, I will track you and the first mistake you make will be your last. You may think this is over, but it's not, your greed will pull you down. I am not working alone, there are many of us and we never forgive and we never forget. Keep an eye on your rear-view mirror, monster, because we're not so far behind and we WILL find you – that's a promise!

THE END

Acknowledgements

With many thanks to my hard working reading panel – Bill, Sue L, Helen, Pauline, Sue P, Erica and Kerry. The Writer's Circle at the Cammarch, and of course, The Book Folks.

If you enjoyed this book, please let others know by leaving a quick review on Amazon. Also, if you spot anything untoward in the paperback, get in touch. We strive for the best quality and appreciate reader feedback.

editor@thebookfolks.com

www.thebookfolks.com

More fiction by Nicola Clifford

NO REFUGE

Reporter Stacey Logan has little to worry about other than the town flower festival when a man is shot dead. When she believes the police have got the wrong man, she does some snooping of her own. But will her desire for a scoop lead her to a place where there is no refuge?

Other titles of interest

The four-book series by Cheryl Rees-Price

Brought up on a hippy commune, DI Winter Meadows is not your ordinary detective. You could guess from his name, really.

But will a cop with a sensitive side have what it takes to police a remote Welsh community with more than its fair share of crime?

Or will he be seen as a soft touch by locals who have all manner of skeletons in the closet?

Pippa McCathie's Welsh mystery series

Having left the police following a corruption investigation, ex-superintendent Fabia Havard is struggling with civilian life. Nonetheless she sets to her new career as an illustrator.

However, when a girl is murdered in her town, old instincts kick in and she is desperate to find the killer. Her former colleague Matt Lambert will have to decide whether to stop her or allow his former boss to assist the floundering inquiry.

So begins a series of cases in which Havard, with her local knowledge and experience, will play a pivotal if unconventional role.

www.thebookfolks.com

Printed in Great Britain
by Amazon

61236943R00149